ALL HEROES ARE HATED

By
MILTON LESSER

ARMCHAIR FICTION
PO Box 4369, Medford, Oregon 97504

*For more information about Armchair Books and products, visit our
website at…*

www.armchairfiction.com

Or email us at…

armchairfiction@yahoo.com

THEY WERE BANNED FROM THE STARS

The planet Earth had a strange way of rewarding its heroes: they put an "S" brand on their heads and hunted them down like packs of mangy dogs!

After a terrible accident in which the entire Fomalhaut system had been destroyed, The interstellar government decreed that Earth was no longer allowed to step foot into deep space—and all of Earth's space voyagers, the "starmen" were blamed. Banished to the hills, the starmen were forced to become bandits, to steal food and supplies needed for survival.

But a wealthy man, an entrepreneur, had a plan. If the starmen would work for him for three years, he would remove the "S" brands from their heads—they would at last be free. But the entrepreneur made one big mistake—he lusted for and took Kenton's wife. And Now Kenton wouldn't rest until he rescued her and escaped to the stars…

FOR A COMPLETE SECOND NOVEL, TURN TO PAGE 77

CAST OF CHARACTERS

KEITH KENTON
With his wife abducted and friends duped, this space pilot was desperate to rescue them—and to get Earth back into space.

VALERIE KENTON
This beautiful girl was willing to leave behind her secure world of prosperity and follow her husband anywhere—even to the stars!

PROFESSOR WILTON
He came from the Antares system, a delegate of the Interstellar Council. His purpose: find a way to get Earth back into space.

BRIAN O'KEEF
He was the bitter XO of the Deneb, and the leader of a banished group of starmen that desperately wanted their lives back

GEORGE BANCROFT
He bore the brand of a starman, but something was amiss—and he had a growing obsession for another man's wife.

ATWELL
This strong, corpulent man came to the starmen with a plan. But was it his plan or someone else's?

HARKNESS
He was the captain of the Deneb and a man who loved his liquor, a love that got him a lot more than he bargained for.

CHAPTER ONE

KENTON knew all along that he should not have come to the city. Morning was coming and the people would see him.

It was an old city, not one of those built by the returned starmen, and its people would hate him. Kenton entered the square but still he saw no one. For a long while he stood at the base of the great bronze statue of the man who had first broken through into space, so many hundreds of years ago. The pre-dawn dusk still hung low over the city and he could not see the face of the statue, but he had seen such statues before and he knew the man's eyes were wide and he was looking up at the sky. It was the pose of a supplicant, a pose Kenton had assumed many times himself. It was meaningless—there was the Sanction and the stars could never be anything more than a speckled backdrop for Kenton's dreams.

Then Kenton saw the sign. It was fastened about one of the massive legs of the figure atop the pedestal, too high for Kenton to reach. It said:

THIS STATUE IS CONDEMNED, DEMOLITION
DATE, AUGUST 7, 2914

August 7th—that was today.

Something inside Kenton went numb. There was nothing in the city for him, nothing to call him back there in the face of all the hatred, except the statue. And now they had marked it for destruction. It was a tribute to the first of the starmen, and they would destroy it. He wondered if they intended to destroy the hundreds of silent ships waiting in the starfield for a day which would never come. This hatred could be a two-way proposition, for suddenly Kenton found himself hating the men of the city.

KENTON looked up uneasily. All at once he knew he was not alone. He did not know where the little man had come from or when he had entered the square, but now he was standing there, his bald head hardly coming to Kenton's shoulders.

"You are a starman?" The little man's voice was not unpleasant, but there was something vaguely familiar about his accent.

Kenton scowled, and his voice was bitter. "You're not guessing, are you?"

"Why, no. No, I'm not. I see the letter *S* on your forehead, and so I know you are a starman."

Kenton put a hand up to his forehead. The worst part of it was that he could not even feel the brand. But it was there—a big black letter *S*. *S* for Starman. *S* like a motionless black snake from his hairline to the bridge of his nose. *S* so that everyone would know to hate him because he was a starman.

"Okay, I'm a starman. Now run along before you get hurt. Starmen hurt people, you know. They go around hurting people all the time. That's how they stay alive. So go away, old man, before you get hurt."

The little man shrugged. "I'm new here. There's a lot that I don't understand yet. But I'm not afraid of you just because you wear an *S* on your forehead. I'd like to help you…"

It had been a long time since anyone had said that, or anything like it, to Kenton. He looked hard at the strange little man. If there had been anyone who wanted to befriend him—wanted to help a starman—it would turn out to be a little man with glasses, a bald head, and a pleasant smile. A harmless, ineffectual creature.

"They're going to take down the statue," Kenton said. "They're going to take it down because they want to forget. It's been only ten years and they haven't forgotten yet, so they're going to take down the statue."

"He was one of you? He was a starman?"

Kenton nodded. "He was the first starman."

"And you are one of the last. It's pathetic in a way. Earth has been ruled out of space, and now the starmen have come back—"

Kenton often thought of this in self-pity, but he had never heard anyone but a starman say it before. Yet this little old man could not be one of them; he was not branded with the black S.

"Who are you?" Kenton demanded.

"Does it matter? I have said I am a stranger in the city, and I am. Consider me as a tourist if you'd like. That's what I am, a tourist."

"Then you must be rich—only the rich travel today. And when the starmen brought the colonists back ten years ago, that doubled Earth's population. Few people are rich. If you were rich you would not wear that shabby clothing. You are no tourist."

"Logical, my boy. That is very logical. You have a good mind. Your argument is valid, it is valid all the way through. But you are wrong, because validity and truth can be two very different things. I am a tourist."

"STARMAN! Hey, look—the black *S*. He's a starman." It was a child's voice, the voice of a twelve-year-old boy, perhaps. It was the only sound except for the sweep of the wind across the starfield just north of the city on the hill. Kenton saw the kid come running into the square from one of the side streets, and then he saw him turn and call back over his shoulder.

"A starman, gang! Let's get him."

Kenton was not surprised to see the dozen kids out this early in the morning. Often they would sneak away from their homes before the sun came up and go out to the eerie starfield and play among the silent hulks of the starships. Kenton could remember his own youth, but it had been different: then he would creep out of bed in the darkest part of night which comes just before dawn and he would run with his friends down to the base of the hill, and there they would watch the great liners taking off for Sirius or Altair or Fomalhaut.

But now the liners lay awkwardly about the field, like huge silver insects that wanted to fly but were wingless, and the wind swept down among them, scaring the kids who came to play every morning...

Kenton heard the stone clatter against the pedestal of the statue and he jumped back and crouched at its base. This was not the first time he had been stoned by children. With the little man he stood in the center of the square, and although now they were crouched behind the pedestal and out of range for the moment, some of the kids could circle around and pelt them from the rear.

The little man seemed unperturbed. "Why are they throwing stones at us?"

"Not at you, old man; not at you. You just happen to be here, but they're throwing stones at me. I'm a starman. I've got an *S* on my forehead."

"But *why* are they throwing stones?"

Kenton mumbled an answer under his breath. He was sorry the little man was with him, but now he could do nothing about it. The rapid tattoo of the stones set up quite a clatter, and he saw some of the kids circling the pedestal.

A stone struck his elbow, numbing his whole arm. He gripped the little man's shoulder. "I'm going to make a run for it," he said. "They're throwing at me, not you—and I'm going to make a run for it. They won't hurt you after that."

The little man put up a hand in protest, and he opened his mouth to say something, but Kenton put his big palm against the man's chest and shoved him back down against the base of the pedestal. Then Kenton stood up and ran.

SOME OF the kids were frightened, and they turned and bolted for the side streets. But one of them was braver; he came close enough to stick out his leg and trip Kenton. Then he whooped triumphantly and called to his companions.

Kenton sprawled there on the pavement, and he saw the kids coming back. He started to get up, but he didn't have to. Someone yanked him to his feet.

The commotion had attracted some adults, and, in dressing gowns or pajamas, they had come running into the square. A big, blunt-faced man was holding Kenton by his numb arm and shaking a hairy fist in his face.

"We don't want you here. We don't want you, starman. What are you doing in this city?"

"He's scaring the kids. Damn him, he's scaring our kids."

"Yeah. He thinks he's hot stuff. A big guy, and he's tough with the kids. We oughta teach him a lesson."

"Why the hell don't you stay in the hills where you belong, starman? Why don't you stay in the hills and leave our kids alone?" This was a woman, and she came close enough to slap Kenton's face. She swung with her full arm and the heel of her palm struck Kenton's jaw. He was still dazed from his fall, and he reeled with the blow, but the blunt-faced man held him up so the woman could hit him again.

She pulled her arm back and this time her fist was clenched. Someone caught her arm before she could strike, and Kenton saw it was the little old man.

"That's enough," he said. "That's quite enough. Stop hitting him."

"Just who do you think you are?" demanded the blunt-faced man. "He's scaring our kids and we're going to teach him a lesson."

"Well, I don't think you ought to hit him. I was here and I saw the children start throwing stones at him. He didn't do anything."

"He didn't do anything! Will you listen to that! He didn't do anything. He's a starman, and because of what he done ten years ago, our kids gotta go hungry. Because of what he done, Earth's got six billion mouths to feed. Because of what he done, we can't ever go back to the stars and get rich again. He didn't do anything—haw, haw."

"I'm new here," explained the little old man, "and I don't know everything that is going on—"

The woman who had struck Kenton frowned. "Well, friend, if you're new here, you better mind your own business. Even if I can't see how you don't know about all this, you better mind your own business. These hicks…"

She pulled her arm out of the old man's grasp and turned again to Kenton. By now a dozen people had struck him, and she leered at his bloody face. Kenton tore himself away from the blunt-faced man and ran through the crowd. On its edge, someone else struck him and he tottered and almost fell, but he knew that if he did fall he would not get up until they were through with him.

THEN HE was through the crowd, still running. Someone grabbed at his jacket and pulled it off his back, and then he had ducked up a side street. Doors were opening now and people were shouting and he could hear the angry muttering of the crowd behind him.

Presently he reached an intersection, where a solitary ground car had paused at a traffic signal. He yanked the door open, and the fat driver grunted, "Hey, what the hell do you want?"

Kenton pulled the man toward him. He hit him once and hit hard and the man's eyes rolled wide and then closed. Kenton pulled him all the way out and let him slump to the pavement. Then he was in the car, studying the controls. The crowd was pounding up to the intersection now, and Kenton hadn't been in a car for ten years. A hand reached at the door and pawed within; then, with a whir, Kenton started the vehicle and left the crowd milling angrily at the intersection.

CHAPTER TWO
The Other Exile

KENTON stood on the edge of the starfield, looking out upon the great silent ships. He should have kept right on going to the hills, he knew, because some of the city dwellers might be following him. Instead, he had circled around the long dimension of the starfield and parked the car on the other side, five miles from the city.

The wind came in fierce blasts, ripping into Kenton's raw face. It moaned fitfully against the hulls of the silent ships—against the *Arcturus*, only Earth ship to reach the Magellanic Clouds; the *Centauri*, first Earth ship to leave the Solar System and return; the *Deneb*, of which Kenton had been the master pilot...

He could remember that day, so many years ago, when he had come straight from Spaceman's School on Luna to the *Deneb*, when he had been twenty-one and everyone had said "Yes, sir, Mr. Kenton," and "No, sir, Mr. Kenton," and when he had taken the great silver ship out for the first time. That was fifteen years ago; now the ship lay on its silver belly among a thousand others as the wind whistled by.

Kenton was not aware that he had been walking until he covered half the distance between the edge of the field and the huge bulk of the *Deneb*. The ship was just in front of him, and a smile tugged at the corners of his mouth. He had been the master pilot, not the captain, but the *Deneb* was *his* ship. He followed its flowing lines with his eyes now: built long and slender not for speed, for it met no resistance in the interstellar void, but for beauty. He could remember that first day going up the ramp in his shiny new uniform and all the smart salutes of the minor officers. Now those officers—if they lived—were starmen with big black *S's* branded on their foreheads, members of the fraternity of hate.

The ramp was there, the same ramp, and Kenton's feet carried him up it again. He wore no jacket, his shirt was torn and his face was cut and bruised, but he walked proudly up the same ramp and reached the *Deneb's* port. He stood there a long while and let the wind buffet him. Then he turned his back on the wind and pushed against the port. Rusty machinery ground in protest, and then Kenton almost fell back off the ramp.

The port had slid open.

His slow measured step was almost reverent as he entered the ship and he could feel his heart pounding hard under the torn shirt. Only a little light came in through the port, and he followed one wall of the companionway with his hand. He headed forward for the engine room, where, if some accident had also left that door open, he might caress the controls and firing studs of the great starship he had once piloted.

The sound his shoes made on the metal floor of the companionway was abnormally loud, and his hands trembled when he reached the door. He stood there for a moment, praying it would open to his touch, and then he gave it a sudden push.

The door stood ajar and the light from the sun, streaming in through the fore-port, blinded him. Then something hurtled against him and he was born to the floor back out in the dark companionway, and he struggled with an unknown assailant.

Tears of rage welled in Kenton's eyes. "Damn you," he muttered. "Damn you!"

IN THE DARKNESS he could not see his attacker, but he fought. The ordeal of the morning had left him weak, and for a while he lay there, the fists pummeling his face and body. Someone sat astride Kenton and was hitting him, but he realized the blows were not hard ones. He pushed up and over and he heard a whimper, and then he was on top, reaching for his assailant's throat.

His hands found the throat and his fingers closed down on it. He leaned forward, exerting pressure, and then, abruptly, he stopped. The faint scent of perfume reached his nostrils—he had not smelled perfume in ten years, but he could not mistake it. As he relaxed his grip, the whimpering came again, and Kenton knew this was no man he fought. He had almost killed a woman.

Stiffly, he stood up and backed away, watching the dim shape rise there in the darkness.

"Okay," the girl panted. "You're big and you're strong and you can beat up a woman. Now I'll go back. "I'll go back to George Bancroft. Now are you satisfied? He must be paying you plenty for this."

Kenton said, "I'm not taking you back anywhere because I don't know where you're supposed to go. I never even heard of George Bancroft. So keep your shirt on."

"Well, if George didn't send you, why did you follow me here? No-one but kids come out among these ships anymore, and all the ships except this one are locked. So why did you follow me?"

"I didn't follow you. I came here because I once piloted the *Deneb*, and I wanted to see it again—"

Kenton was sorry as soon as he had spoken. Now the girl would know he was a starman.

"You piloted the *Deneb?*"

Kenton muttered "yes" under his breath.

"Then you're a starman!" Kenton found himself liking the sound of her voice. He was used to the coarse women at the starmen camps in the hills, and this girl sounded different. "A starman—and I know you. You're Keith Kenton."

"Yes, I'm Kenton..." His voice trailed off. How had she known? No one hob-nobbed with the starmen; no one came near them except in hatred. Yet she knew his name.

"Hah!" she said. "You're surprised that I know you. Don't be, Kenton. I've studied history; I know my starmen. Keith Kenton, Master Pilot, Starship *Deneb*, born 2878, graduated Luna 2899, five years a pilot, then came back to Earth with the Sanction in 2904. Keith Kenton."

"You have an advantage. I don't even know your name."

The girl laughed again, and suddenly Kenton did not care if he got into the engine room or not. He wanted to go outside with this girl and see her there on the ramp with the wind blowing in her hair. He didn't know how he knew, but he knew she'd be lovely.

He reached for her hand and she drew away from him. "Careful, Kenton. You're right, you don't know me. Please don't start getting impetuous. I've had enough of impetuous men."

Now Kenton laughed, and he had not heard the sound of his own laughter in a long time. "Nothing like that. I'm too tired. I just wanted to take your hand so we could walk down the companionway together and go outside where I can see you."

He was conscious of the silence, and then he heard the girl's voice again. "All right, Kenton."

The girl's hand took his in the darkness. He liked the feel of it.

THEY STOOD at the foot of the ramp and Kenton looked at the girl. He looked a long time and she said, "Stop it, I'll blush."

Her skin was very white and she had the greenest eyes in the world. The wind swept her dark hair around her face and where the sun touched it, the highlights were red. Kenton's gaze moved down. She wore a tunic of pale green, custom-tailored and glove-perfect in its fit. Her legs were long and straight, very white where the skirt ended at mid-thigh. Kenton realized he had not yet let go of her hand.

For her part, the girl stared at Kenton. Mostly her eyes remained rooted to the black S on his forehead.

"You know," she said, "I've never seen a starman before."

"It isn't odd," Kenton admitted. "It's not odd at all." Then he asked a question: "Are you a colonist or a Terran?"

"Oh, I'm Terran. If I were a colonist, I'd have returned to Earth in '04, and I'd have seen my starman then. No, I'm a Terran, but sometimes I look at the stars and I wish—"

She stopped, and Kenton just looked at her. Then she said: "I wish there was no Sanction. I wish I was—"

This time she turned away, and she said, "You'll only make fun of me, Kenton."

"I won't make fun of you."

"I wish I were out there among the stars. I don't like the Earth, Kenton, I don't like it at all. There's not much I can do about it, and I've never been anywhere else and so I can't be sure, but I think I would like it better. You've been…everywhere, Kenton."

He smiled. "You would like it better. You'd like it much better. The Earth is a tired planet—a luxury planet once, a pleasure planet. But now it's a hard place to live. The population is doubled, and half the people are unemployed. Then there are us starmen…"

"Why do they hate you so, Kenton? Oh, I know the reason, but why is there so *much* hatred?" She put her hand on the black *S,* ran her fingers soothingly over his forehead.

Kenton smiled slightly. This was the second time today someone had shown sympathy. First the little old man there in the square, and now this girl. Ordinarily, Kenton was not talkative. But now he wanted to, because he knew the girl would listen.

THEY WALKED in silence for a while, past the *Arcturus* and past the *Centauri.* She looked up at him—again her eyes strayed to the *S* and stayed there, and he saw pity in them. "Why, Kenton? I've asked you a question. Tell me why."

Kenton's answer was another question. "What's your name?"

"Why don't we leave it this way? I'll walk with you until it gets dark. I'll walk with you long into the night if you want. But don't ask me who I am. I'll walk with you and be your friend, Kenton, but don't ask me my name."

"Why not?"

"Just don't, that's all."

Kenton said lightly. "Okay, okay, I won't. But don't you go around asking me questions."

"Please, Kenton, you're being unfair. You don't know *why* I can't tell you my name, but it's not just a whim. I can't tell you because I don't want you to know who you've been with."

"I never would have known it." Kenton could feel himself getting bitter again, and he tried to tell himself how unimportant her name really was, but he knew he wanted her to tell him.

She smiled, but now she let go of his hand. "You're pushing me, Kenton, and I don't want to be pushed. Look, maybe I'm trying to get away from someone, and maybe, if you should be asked, I don't want you to be able to say you saw me. Maybe I'm running away, too."

Kenton looked again at her clothing. It was a delicate fabric, an expensive fabric. Even this soon after the Sanction there were few rich people left on Earth, but he knew this girl was rich.

"They hate you enough to beat you, Kenton. That's what happened to your face, isn't it? Your face doesn't look so good, Kenton."

"What's the difference? Very few people look at it. We starmen aren't exactly social lions."

"I was fifteen when the Sanction came, Kenton. That was ten years ago. I read the papers and listened to the reports. But I was a kid, and didn't really understand. And now everyone hates you starmen, but I don't hate you. You did something wrong. Maybe you did something terribly wrong—ten years ago. All of you didn't do it, though."

Kenton said, "It was done, all right, and now Earth has six billion people. Not three billion, spread out all over the planet and living off the luxuries of the star-trade. But six billion, and that's a lot of people. Six billion, with not enough jobs for half of them.

"Maybe the colonists hate us even worse than you Terrans do. Earth is not for the colonists, but they were forced to return. Now they're out of place, and most of them are out of work."

"I was almost a colonist, Kenton. I remember, just before the Sanction, we were going to the Vegan System. I had an uncle there, and he was getting Dad a job, a good job. But the Sanction came and now my uncle's back on Earth. He's been unemployed for ten years, and once he found a starman getting food from our cook. He killed the man. He killed him and a lot of people saw it, yet no one did anything. They shouldn't be able to go around killing—"

"The old laws don't apply. Oh, they apply to Terrans and they apply to colonists, but they don't apply to starmen. There are only a couple of hundred thousand of us, and the old laws don't apply. If the people had their way, we'd all be killed. But they don't, because it's just possible that one day the Sanction will be lifted, and then the starmen will be needed to take Earth's millions back into space again.

"Instead we wear the black S, so everyone will know we are starmen, and we can't get jobs anywhere. Then the people say, 'See the shiftless starmen.' And a lot of us become outlaws…"

"Were you ever an outlaw?" she asked.

"I have to eat. I haven't had much to do with the bands in the hills, but I have to eat."

THE GIRL turned around and faced him, and Kenton was lost for a moment in the depths of her eyes. Above them, the sun was low on the horizon now, and the cold winds had begun to blow again over the starfield, moaning past the silent hulks of the starships. They were in the middle of the starfield, and it stretched from one horizon to the other, except where Kenton could see the city on the hill way off in the distance. It stretched out in all directions, barren and brooding, more a graveyard than any cemetery Kenton ever had seen.

Slim fingers dug into Kenton's shoulder, and the girl's face was close to his. "What really happened?" she said. "What happened out in the Fomalhaut System ten years ago? Tell me, Keith." It was the first time she had used his given name.

Kenton frowned. She was a wealthy girl with wealthy friends, and maybe she just wanted him to tell her so she could tell all her friends about the day she had spent with a starman. Once on the *Deneb* a girl had spent the whole voyage with him, laughing and drinking and dancing. But she met her fiancé in the Centauri System, and as they walked away Kenton had heard her speaking of all she had learned from the Master Pilot. Now, again, it was a girl on the *Deneb*, the silent hulk of the *Deneb*, only this time she had come off the ship with Kenton. There was no one else and she had come off the ramp all alone with Kenton.

"IT WAS the *Deneb*," Kenton said. "It was the *Deneb* out in the Fomalhaut System, and I was there."

"Keith—you saw it. The histories never say which ship was responsible; they only tell what happened, not how or why. You were there…"

"We had come through to Fomalhaut in record time, six days. Everyone celebrated. Six days was quick, all the way out to Fomalhaut, and we had a wild party to celebrate. Some of the men got drunk. We all got drunk, but some of us got too drunk.

"The Captain couldn't hold his liquor. He couldn't hold it at all, and he should have known. We were waiting for clearance out of hyper-space, but the Captain became impatient. He blasted out too soon and we were close to Fomalhaut, and someone forgot to lock the hyperdrive. We came through into space with both drives going.

"Do you know what the hyperdrive can do to a star? We couldn't shut it in time—the Captain had locked himself in the control room, and some of us knew because the stasis was still going, but we couldn't get in. Do you know what the hyperdrive can do?"

Kenton could feel the tears in his eyes, and the wind stung him. The girl said: "There are the histories, but they don't tell much—"

"It can knock hell out of a star. Fomalhaut is a big baby, but the hyperdrive is a pretty powerful thing—it can shoot you across the galaxy to the Magellanic Clouds in a few years. It took us to Fomalhaut in six days, record time. And we switched out of hyper-space too soon, without clearance, with the hyperdrive going full blast.

"We broiled Fomalhaut. In a few seconds, we turned it into a supernova. In a month it had used up the energy stored there for billions of years of future use. We high-tailed it back into hyper-space and we weren't touched. But Fomalhaut...

"Fomalhaut had six planets. Six planets and twelve billion inhabitants. They were a slow people, several hundred years behind Earth in development. They had interplanetary travel, crude stuff, but they never got out of their own System. They roasted. Every one of them roasted. In a matter of days, the twelve billion inhabitants of the Fomalhaut System were dead, and we had killed them…"

Kenton was crying openly now. The tears were rolling down his cheeks, but no sound came out of him. They had sat down on one of the many ramps, and the girl drew his head down on her breast. "I'm sorry, Keith," she said. "I'm really sorry. I shouldn't have made you talk."

HE SMILED and straightened up. "No. No, it's good. I've got to get it out, and the way we live now, I can't. But *twelve billion* people! They weren't exactly human, but they were people—you get to feel that way when you're a starman. Twelve billion people, and we killed them. They never had a chance.

"The Interstellar Government met in special session. It hardly ever meets, you know—only in a real emergency. They met, and to a man, they voted Earth out of space. We weren't ready, we were too young and there was too much danger. It wasn't likely, but something like that *could* happen again. One chance in a million, maybe less—but they didn't want to take the responsibility, and Earth was ruled out of space. Confined to the Solar System, which is a laugh—because Earth alone can harbor life here.

"So, after the Sanction, the starmen came back. We brought the colonists with us. They had no choice, either. They were exiled back to Earth, every last one of them. And Earth had lived on the luxury trade of the star-lanes. All the really big cities were gone, and Earth couldn't support six billion people. It had to, it's doing it now but in ten years the standard of living dropped five-hundred percent. The roof fell in, and it hasn't hit the ground yet."

The girl nodded. "So the starmen are to blame."

"Yes. And in a sense, they're right. The qualifications on Spaceman's School entrance should have been more rigid. I don't know. We're to blame, and we're branded, so everyone will know."

"And no one on Earth—except your crew—has ever seen what happened to Fomalhaut."

"I hadn't thought of that. But you're right, of course. Fomalhaut is a lot more than ten light years away, and it still shines as if nothing has happened. Suddenly, years from now, it will flare up—"

"Maybe by then the people will forget."

"They'll never forget. No one can marry a starman. It's forbidden. Women are taken in the hills, of course, but the starmen are dying out. The people will forget in another fifty years, when there are no starmen left, but not before. Meanwhile we can only die…"

"You could go into space! Unlawfully, you could go into space."

Kenton smiled ruefully. "No. There's the Sanction, and they have monitors. In the beginning, a few of the starmen tried, but they were blasted out of space. We're Earthbound. The whole culture is Earthbound with nothing to do. It's as if the stars don't exist. And we're going backwards. Civilization is collapsing. It's hard to see in ten years, but with all this unemployment, all the discontent—Earth is on the way down.

"I met a guy today. He was a tourist. I don't know where he was from but he was a tourist. That's rare; there just aren't many tourists any more. There's no time, there's no money, and few people want to do that sort of thing.

Once you've been to the stars you can't be content with one stinking little planet in a System of eight other worlds, all dead..."

THE SUN had set and now the stars were out. It was a clear night with no moon, and the great white arc of the Milky Way spanned the sky mockingly. The liners were huge dark shadows on the star field, and off in the distance the lights of the city on the hill could not dim the stars. The wind didn't hurt Kenton's face anymore—he could feel the stiffness where blood had clotted.

The girl seemed perfectly content to walk with him and say nothing, and Kenton felt more at ease than he had in the past ten years. Once they looked up together, spontaneously, at the stars, and Kenton thought of the statue in the square. According to schedule, it had been destroyed today.

Suddenly they heard the distant whir of an automobile motor. The girl said: "They're looking for me."

Kenton couldn't argue with that. He didn't know why the girl was out here on the star field, but he did know that she was running away from something. And no one—except kids, who didn't drive ground cars—came out to the starfield anymore.

The sound grew louder, and presently Kenton saw a great fanning search-beam rove over the shapes of the deserted liners. Not more than a few hundred feet could be between them and the car now, and the girl huddled close to Kenton as the beam swept near them. They tried to duck down beneath one of the ramps, and for a moment Kenton thought they had made it. But the beam cut sharply back, probing the darkness under the ramp.

Soon the whir of the engine stopped altogether, and the silence which followed hurt Kenton's ears. He could feel the girl trembling beside him, and he put his arm across her shoulder, clumsily. Then he heard footsteps in the darkness under the ramp, just beyong where the beam could reach.

"Come on, get out of there," the voice said. It wasn't a loud voice, but it was loud enough, and Kenton recognized the ring of authority when he heard it.

"I know you're there, so come on, get out. Now."

They were under the ramp, and here the ramp was three feet off the ground. In the light of the beam from the car, Kenton saw the legs. There were four legs—two men—and they were close. Then one pair of legs bent at the knees, and a new light, a strong and blinding light, knifed in under the ramp.

The voice again: "Okay, I see you. Now, come out."

KENTON took his arm away from the girl's shoulders. This wasn't his fight, and maybe those two men had a gun. He crawled until he had gotten out from under the ramp, and then he stood up, the light shining in his face and blinding him. A sound from behind him indicated the girl was coming out, too.

The voice, this time close by, said, "Do you see that? Do you see what I see? I don't know who he is, but he's with her and he's wearing the black *S*. *He*'s a starman. Now what would she be doing with one of them?"

The other voice was softer, and Kenton could tell that the man didn't want to say much. "You never can tell what Valerie will do. Here's Valerie, and there's nothing amazing about her being with a starman."

The girl said quietly, "Hello, George. Okay, you found me. But I don't want to go back with you."

The softer voice belonged to George. "You haven't much choice, Valerie. You'll come back with me."

Kenton said: "The lady said she doesn't want to go."

The deeper voice, the voice that wasn't George Bancroft's, answered: "Watch it, starman. This is none of your business, and it could get you killed. No one would care, you know."

"I'd care," the girl told him. "Don't hurt him."

"Okay, okay." This was George, and he still held the light so Kenton could not see. "So you'll care. We won't hurt him. We'll let him go back to the hills where he belongs. But you're coming with me now, Valerie."

"There's only one thing you don't seem to understand."

"Yes? What's that?"

"I don't want to marry you, George. I don't want to marry you, now or ever. I'll go back to the city if you force me to, but I won't marry you. Do you understand that?"

In answer, a hand came into view and grabbed the girl's shoulder. She tried to pull away, but the hand was strong and her struggles were useless.

Kenton swung the side of his own hand down in a hard chopping blow against the man's wrist. The hand retreated into the darkness, and George's voice said: "Take care of him. Take care of the starman."

Into the light came the big bulk of the other man, but Kenton hit him before he could get ready. Kenton hit him just once, but the man moaned and fell slowly out of the light.

Kenton heard an angry oath from George, and the beam of light did a crazy dance upwards and then came down fast, and Kenton realized George was trying to hit him with the torch. Kenton lunged down and away and the light swung past and he struck out blindly behind it and felt his knuckles brush against George's face. Then they were in close, slugging at each other, and this George could punch. It was so dark that Kenton could see nothing. The light fell and went out, and someone shut off the fanning beam in the car, probably the girl.

George began to falter. Kenton kept on punching, but he had to lower his blows or he would be striking at air. He felt the bulk of George's weight at his knees, and he had a wild temptation to kick out with his leg. Only it wasn't necessary. George Bancroft had had enough, and now he slumped all the way to the ground and lay still.

Kenton stood there, panting. Then the fanning light from the car went on again, and the engine started, drowning out the sound of the wind.

The car crawled over to Kenton and stopped. The girl was at the controls.

"Let's go," she said. "Get in."

CHAPTER THREE
The Hunted Ones

IT WAS a nice day, a warm spring day, and up on the other side of the hills the wind was not as strong. They had abandoned the ground car at the foot of the hills because it was not made to travel over rough terrain, and they had made their way up and over the hills on foot. Now they were hungry. Three days had passed; and while they could satisfy their thirst in the mountain streams, the berries and fruits they ate were not enough to satisfy their hunger.

When Kenton was still a boy, he would come to these hills, because from the very highest point you could look down on the starfield and see the tiny dots of ships as they took off. Now the ships didn't take off anymore, and Kenton and the girl had already passed that high point and kept going. Kenton wanted to put as much distance as possible between them and the city.

Here, on the third day, the girl noticed the extent of wilderness for the first time. "Kenton, there are no people. It's deserted. With, six billion people on Earth, how can that be?"

He laughed shortly. "You forget that the starmen take to the hills, but they stay near enough to the cities so that they can raid for food and women. People give the starmen a wide range—no one wants any part of 'em unless they come down to the cities, and then there's trouble."

"So there are starmen in these hills?"

"Yes. Here, somewhere, there's a big camp of them, perhaps the biggest. Don't you worry your pretty little head, Valerie, they'll find us."

"What are you laughing about? They'll find us—and what will they do?"

"Don't worry. Don't forget, I'm a starman, too. They won't do a thing—and we'll get food."

"We'd better. I'm beginning to feel that there isn't an ounce of flesh on me."

"You don't look it. Besides, I didn't like the idea of you coming up here with me. But then you didn't want to marry the guy."

"What do you mean, me coming up here with you? Who got the car?" Valerie laughed musically, then sobered abruptly. "I didn't have any choice, Keith. George has everything my family wants, and they want me to marry him. I couldn't. We don't get along on anything. We disagree on the most basic things. He probably hates starmen more than anyone else in the city. I mean it, Keith, he probably does. And I—"

"What about you?"

"I don't hate starmen at all. I've only met one, and I don't hate them at all. Keith…"

He took her in his arms and kissed her. For a long while they stood together, close together and her lips were warm and soft and Kenton didn't want to stop kissing her, ever. She pushed him away, slowly, and she was smiling.

Her voice was tremulous: "Keith, I never have to go out of the hills. I could stay here with you and—"

"Sure, sure. How would we live? It's not for you, Valerie. It can never be for you."

He knew he also should have said that it couldn't be because he was a starman. But he didn't say that. Instead he turned and walked away. In the silence he heard the girl moving through the undergrowth behind him. He began to whistle. It was the first time he had whistled in years, he realized. It was a song that had been popular during one of his last flights on the *Deneb*.

WHEN Valerie heard the sounds she told Kenton they were being followed, but he shook his head. No one would come on foot looking for them in the hills. If George was looking for them, it would be in an aircraft.

Yet the sounds were there, for Kenton heard them too. They were not the only one crashing through the thick undergrowth. Kenton said: "The starmen have found us."

Valerie shuddered a little, and Kenton took her hand. "You'd think they'd be quiet about it," she said. "But they're clumping through the woods like a bunch of kids on a picnic. I'm scared, Keith."

"What have they got to be quiet about? No one comes up into these hills, unless he's a starman. Or unless he's running away from something. In the camps here you'll find a few men who don't wear the black *S*. They're here because they can't go back to the cities, and the starmen are glad to have any additions."

"I'm scared, Keith," she said again.

"Take it easy, Val. You've got nothing to be scared about. The starmen are hated, but they don't really hate in return. At least most of them don't. Actually, they're a little afraid, and they keep to themselves except when they venture down to the cities for supplies.

"For supplies? Who sells it to them?"

Kenton laughed. "No one sells them anything. They take what they want, and then they beat it back to the hills. It's only been ten years, but a lot of people in your cities have never seen a starman."

"Um, yes. I've heard mothers make their children behave by saying 'The starman will get you if you're bad.' Did you know that you were a bogey-man, Keith?"

Kenton was about to answer, but he heard a drone from far off. Immediately, the sounds in the woods about them ceased, and the droning became louder. Soon a speck appeared on the horizon back in the direction of the city. It grew larger, and presently Kenton could make out a gyro-plane, a solitary little flying ship approaching from the city.

"That's George," Valerie said.

Kenton grunted as he watched the craft grow. The droning became louder, and soon the ship was directly overhead, not more than two or three hundred feet above the wooded hills. It came so close that Kenton could see the license number on the gray bottom, then passed and droned on until it became a dot in the sky. Then it was gone.

"That's George," Valerie said again. "I know his license number."

"Well, he didn't find anything. He's out looking for you, but he didn't find anything. It won't be easy for him, here in the hills."

She said: "He's still looking."

AND THEN she was silent. The noises had started again in the woods, and soon Kenton could see the men coming through the undergrowth. There were perhaps a dozen of them, and all wore remnants of their uniforms, as did Kenton. They approached easily, confidently, not at all worried by the appearance of two strangers, and presently one of them said: "Kenton? You're Keith Kenton, aren't you?"

Kenton had lived alone instead of with the bands of starmen in the hills, so he did not at first recognize the man. He was big and burly and his hair was very dark, with a dark tangle of beard covering his face. What was left of his uniform showed that he was a captain.

More than anything, it was the bushy black hair which told Kenton who the man was. Ten years slipped away, and Kenton almost found himself coming to attention smartly and saluting. "Captain Harkness," he said, and there was emotion in his voice.

Harkness had been captain of the *Deneb*. It was Harkness who, that terrible day in the Fomalhaut System, could not hold his liquor. Harkness...

"—wondering about you, Kenton," Harkness was saying. "Almost all the old crew of the *Deneb* is together here. Only you, and Denton, and Farley—"

"Farley is dead," Kenton said. "I saw him killed." He had been living in the hills with Farley in the beginning, but one day they had gone down to the city and Farley was killed. That was a long time ago, and until now he had almost forgotten the incident completely.

But the sight of these men made everything come back in a rush. Captain Harkness, Jenkins, O'Keef, Larkin, Finer—they were all there. The men of the *Deneb*. The proud officers of the *Deneb*, living now in the hills like savages. The cream of Earth's culture—or they wouldn't have been starmen—reduced to this. He remembered the day Farley had been killed. They had gone down to the city to get some books—Farley couldn't go for long without Chaucer and Proust and Hemmingway and a lot of the other ancients—and he had been killed getting those books.

Now Jenkins and O'Keef and Larkin were thumping him on the back and smiling at him, and he stripped the beards away with his mind, and how easily the years went with them! There was Larkin pouring over his astrogation charts, flame-haired O'Keef, the exec, thundering his orders down to the 'low decks crew, shy little Jenkins showing some passengers through the communications room...

NOW THEY stood around him in old and filthy clothing, in torn clothing, with beards on their jowls and bangs on their foreheads to hide the black *S*. They all came and they pounded Kenton's back and shook his hand and they jabbered about him excitedly. All except Harkness—after the first happy greeting, Harkness hung back, and Kenton gestured to him now.

"What's the matter with him? He's your leader, isn't he?"

"Harkness?" Larkin snorted. "Harkness, our leader? Hell, no. No one pays much attention to Harkness now. He hardly ever talks. He said hello to you, and that's amazing. That's probably all you'll get out of him—"

"Oh, he *talks*." This was little Jenkins. "But better not pay too much attention to what he says. Our leader? Well, that's Brian here." And he pounded big O'Keef in the ribs.

O'Keef grinned affably. "I'm glad to have you back with us, Keith, boy. Even if you are a Scot." And then he was laughing, and it was the old, familiar humorous bone of contention that had always been between them, as it was ten years ago, and Kenton knew that the big smiling O'Keef had not changed much.

"Mister Kenton! Mister Kenton!" It was a voice Kenton remembered well, and again, he had the odd feeling that he should jump to attention.

Captain Harkness approached him. "We're set to blast off, Mister, so what are you standing around for? Get set, Mister, because we're ready to blast off for Fomalhaut." His face was very serious.

"Oh, Lord," Larkin said. "He's going to Fomalhaut again. It isn't so bad when he goes anyplace else, but when he goes to Fomalhaut he just keeps talking and talking—"

"You there, Larkin, got that orbit mapped?"

Larkin snapped to attention. "Yes, sir. All right now, sir. On the beam all the way." He nudged Kenton with his elbow, but Kenton knew that Larkin wasn't so tough. He was not humoring Harkness to be funny. He felt sorry for the man.

Harkness shouted his orders around in the voice that Kenton remembered so well, and presently O'Keef said:

"All right now, sir. We're underway. We can take it easy for a while."

Harkness smiled. "You think so, Mister O'Keef? You think it was a good blast-off?"

"It was perfect," O'Keef assured him.

VALERIE HAD stood on the edge of the little clearing, not saying a word, and it was the first time, Kenton realized, that his thoughts had been off her for more than a few moments since they had met.

"Hey, Val," he called, and smiling a bit shyly, she approached. Kenton introduced her around and she nodded to everyone and Kenton told them that this was his woman. He waited for Valerie to deny it—he almost expected her to do so, but then he knew that she'd understand this was the best way. By telling them she was his woman, no one would bother her.

They all nodded and they smiled and they shook Valerie's hand as if she were a man. All except Harkness. Harkness wanted to know what a woman was doing hob-nobbing with the crew.

Kenton was still talking about old times as they walked toward the camp, talking with Jenkins and Larkin, O'Keef and Finer, talking of the old days when they were the rollicking crew of the *Deneb*. They were the rollicking happy-go-lucky crew of the *Deneb*, the laughing crew of one of the biggest, proudest space liners in the fleet. And now they wore beards, and they wore bangs because they didn't want to be reminded of the black *S* on each of their foreheads, and the captain still gave his orders here on Earth in the hills beyond the field where the *Deneb* waited silently, and no one listened to him…

CHAPTER FOUR
The Offer

THERE WERE some things about the camp in the hills which Kenton liked, and for a time at least he was sorry he had not spent those last ten years there. Actually, though, it was hard to tell. He was happier now than he had been in a decade, but he knew that Valerie, as much as anything, was responsible for that. Best of all he liked to sit high on a hill at night with the girl at his side and watch the great sweep of stars overhead and dream that one day he would be out there again, in all that splendor, and this time the girl would be with him.

Several times in those weeks which followed, Kenton heard the far-off drone of aircraft, but only twice did a ship actually come close enough for them to see it. The first time it was George again, and he swooped down low over the camp and Kenton could not tell if he had seen it or not. The shacks were of wood, roofs covered with branches and shrubbery, built about the big clearing haphazardly. From the air they should look like so many trees or clumps of trees, Kenton thought. And that, of course, was the idea. The starmen wanted it this way; they wanted the location of their camp a secret. Brian O'Keef had told Kenton about that the first day. The smile had gone from the eyes of the flame-topped giant as he told Kenton that you'd never know when the city-dwellers would take it upon themselves to comb the hills for the starmen.

The second airship was not George's. Even from a distance they could tell it was much too big, and when it came close Kenton saw that the license number was different. The ship hovered over the camp for a long time, its gyro-blades gleaming in the sun, then it dipped once and headed back toward the city. O'Keef didn't like that. He didn't like that at all. The unknown pilot, Kenton thought, had certainly seen the campsite for what it was.

After that, there were no more forays into the city. The starmen had enough of everything for a while: their provisions weren't luxurious, but Kenton had had much worse—he had lived on much worse for ten years, and he found it no hardship to remain in the clearing.

ONE DAY NOT long after the second airship had come and gone, Valerie, laughing mysteriously, led him to a hut a little larger than the rest.

There a man met them at the doorway and, smiling, ushered them in. Then he stood back in the shadows of the interior and he waited, and presently Valerie spoke.

"Keith, do you want to continue to sleep on the floor forever? I sleep in the bed in our shack and you sleep on the floor, and sometimes I feel sorry for you."

"Well, thanks, Val—but I certainly wouldn't want to change places with you. You're a woman—"

"I'm glad you think so, I was wondering. So I'm a woman, Keith…and are you a man?"

"Now, what kind of a question is that?"

The gray-haired man stepped out of the shadows, and the black *S* on his forehead stood out sharply under the gray shock of hair. "Let me introduce myself," he said. "Then maybe you'll see what this young lady is driving at.

I was the chaplain aboard the *Arcturus*. I'm still a chaplain—"

"Oh," said Kenton. "Oh…"

"Now do you get the idea, Keith? Never mind that question. I'll ask another one. Keith, do you love me? Tell me, because if you don't—"

"If I don't—what?" But Kenton was smiling as he took her in his arms, kissing her hair, her lips, her neck, and she was laughing and crying at the same time, and Kenton might have stayed with her that way all day, but the chaplain cleared his throat. As if on a signal, O'Keef and Larkin and Jenkins and a dozen other men came in, and a few women, and then the chaplain began the ceremony…

It wasn't a long ceremony, and Kenton was in pretty much of a daze all the way through. But when it was over he felt very much married, and he shook hands all around and everyone kissed Valerie until Kenton finally grabbed her and took her outside, where he did some kissing himself.

LATER THAT same day, George Bancroft came to the camp. This time there was no aircraft. George came suddenly and he came on foot, and the most surprising thing of all was the fact that he had a big black *S* on his forehead.

Kenton had been talking with Brian O'Keef in his shack, and as he came outside into the sunlight he saw Valerie arguing with someone. Kenton couldn't hear her words, but he could see her frowning, and the man's back was to him. He hurried over and stood beside Valerie, and the man was young and good-looking and Kenton recognized the soft voice as George's. But this was all wrong—the man had a black *S* on his forehead.

"Yes, Keith, it's George all right. You met under different circumstances last time. Mr. Bancroft, Mr. Kenton."

George nodded curtly, and Kenton said: "I didn't know you were a starman. I fought with you in the darkness that night on the starfield, but I didn't know you were a starman. Val never told me."

"He's not," Valerie said. "He never had the mark on his forehead before, and I've known him all my life. George is no starman."

George laughed. "Who said I'm not a starman? I have the black *S* on my forehead, so how can you say I'm not a starman?"

Kenton couldn't understand it. He had to believe Valerie, of course. If Valerie said George was not a starman, then he wasn't. But no one in his right mind would be branded with the black *S;* no one would submit himself to certain ostracism for no apparent reason. Then George must have a reason, he thought.

Valerie said, "He wanted to be a starman. Twelve years ago when the best blood on Earth wanted to join the space fraternity, George wanted to be a starman. We were kids and we were friends then, and I remember how happy George was planning for it."

George scowled. "That's enough, Valerie."

"No, it's not enough. He planned for it and he dreamed of little else. But when he went to Luna to take the test at Spaceman's School, he couldn't make the grade. Psychologically unstable, they said, and George came back to Earth. He's hated the starmen since then; even before the Sanction he hated them. So he had a head start on everyone else, and that's why he hates you so much now. Isn't that right, George?"

"Shut up, Valerie. It's purely by accident that I came here. That is. I came here on purpose, but I didn't know you were here. I came here to do a job and I'm going to do it, and when I'm through I'm going to take you back to the city and we'll be married."

KENTON laughed, "It's against the city law for a girl to marry a starman. Didn't you know that, George? It's against the law."

"I won't be a starman then," George assured him. "This black mark can come off, after it serves its purpose."

Kenton was about to ask him what purpose that was, but Valerie said: "I won't be able to marry you anyway. I'd be a bigamist. Kenton and I were married today. I'm Mrs. Kenton." She put her arm around Kenton's waist and she smiled up at him, and Kenton watched George's face flush an ugly crimson.

"We'll see about that," he said. "We'll see about it. As Kenton admitted, it isn't legal."

"It's legal enough. A chaplain performed the ceremony, and since we're going to live among the starmen, it's legal enough. Look, George, don't bother us; my husband doesn't like to be bothered, so please go away."

Again George laughed. "Why should I go away? I'm a starman and this is the starman camp."

A shadow loomed up near them, and Kenton looked into the smiling face of Brian O'Keef. "Hello, Brian," he said. "Here—"

"I see we have a new recruit, Kenton. Lord, how we can use him. Another arm to raid the city for us. What ship, lad?"

George smiled, and Kenton had to admit it was a winning smile. "I'm afraid I'm pretty much of a stranger.

Name is George Bancroft. But you have no one here of the *Altair's* crew, do you?"

"No. Afraid we don't."

"Well, that's what I thought. I was the exec of the *Altair,* but I can't seem to find any of the crew in the hills. I'll live here if you let me—"

"Let you!" O'Keef roared. "We wouldn't let you get away! We can use men, son, we can use men. The *Altair,* eh?"

"Don't let him fool you, Brian," Kenton said. "I don't know what he wants here or why he's wearing the *S,* but this man is no starman. Ask my wife."

"He's not," Valerie said. "I've known him for years."

Brian smiled, and the grin was meant to be friendly, but it looked like a gargoyle-mask on his battered face. "You must be mistaken, ma'am. You have to be mistaken. Not a starman—that's crazy."

KENTON realized that it *did* sound crazy. It was ridiculous—no man in his right mind would wear the brand of a starman unless it were forced on him in the Sanction. Yet George wore it, and Valerie claimed George was no starman. How could you prove it? Kenton knew that you couldn't.

"—met this man," George was telling the grinning O'Keef. "It sounded like a good proposition, too, and I intended to take him up on it. I haven't run across him again, and that's why I'm here. But he said he'd be in the hills, visiting the camps, and when he comes here, I'm going with him."

Kenton had missed the first part of what George was saying, but he could see that O'Keef was jubilant. "Did you hear that, Keith, lad? Did you hear it?"

Kenton was suddenly very weary. He knew that George was up to something, but that he could do nothing about it. "No," he said. "I didn't hear. What, Brian?"

Valerie said, "Are you crazy? Are you both crazy? This man is not a starman. I know him. I've known him all my life. You've met him too, Kenton. You know he's not a starman."

"Sure," Kenton agreed. "But prove it. How can you prove it?"

"You're mistaken," O'Keef said patiently. "You have to be mistaken."

"Of course," George agreed, smiling. "The lady is thinking of someone else. Perhaps someone who looks like me. It doesn't take much to tell I'm a starman."

"Naturally," O'Keef said. "Naturally. But that's not the important thing. The important thing is what you said.

"How would you like to have that S removed, Kenton? How would you like to live again like a normal human being because there won't be anything to set you apart? How would you like to live without the brand of hate on your forehead where everyone can see it? How would you like that black mark removed, Kenton? Tell me, how would you like it?"

"I would love it," Kenton said, and he meant it.

"Well, Mr. Bancroft here knows a man who can do it! Don't you, Mr. Bancroft? That's what you said, isn't it?"

George nodded. "That's what I said. Of course, I can't be sure, because I only met the man once. But that's what he told me. I'm to work for him for three years. It's hard labor and he told me not to expect anything easy. But I'm to work for him for three years and then he removes the S from my forehead and I'm a free man. I'd break my back for *twenty* years for that. But just to work for three years, and then I'm free! Three years—"

"How about that, Kenton?" O'Keef demanded. "How about that? Valerie, your children won't have to be born and raised here in the hills. Kenton can work for three years like all of us, and he won't be a starman any longer. The black mark will be removed and he won't be a starman any longer. How about that?"

EVERYONE liked it. Everyone in the village loved it. They were so eager to believe it could happen that they took the unsupported word of this man, this stranger with the mark of the starman on his forehead. In a week George had won everyone over. In a week the whole camp had changed. For ten years they had been waiting and dreaming, as Kenton had been waiting and dreaming, for the time when the Sanction would be lifted and the great liners would rise again from the silent starfield. Then they would be there in their bright new uniforms, they would all be there, walking up the ramps two by two while the bands were playing, ready to take their people back into space again.

Now all that was changed. They didn't think in those terms anymore. Now they waited for the coming of the man who could remove the black mark from their foreheads, and then they wouldn't be starmen. They didn't want to be starmen—they had had enough, and now they waited for the man who could take the mark of their identity away from them.

The first day, Kenton tried in vain to reason with them. The black *S* told them clearly enough that George was a starman, a member of the *Altair's* crew, and they wouldn't believe Kenton. He gave up after a day, and even Valerie stopped trying after the second day. That night they went out to their hill and looked up to the stars and the Milky Way was a wonderful bridge to something better, if only they could reach it. Kenton wanted to grasp out with his hands and pull it down, he wanted to take Valerie out to the stars with him. Soon he would be waiting alone. If George had his way, he would be waiting all alone.

It was exactly one week after the arrival of George that Kenton heard the droning. It was a sound he had not heard in ten years, and for a moment he thought a starship was up there someplace in the sky. But then he saw the huge swarm of dots on the horizon and realized a fleet of aircraft was approaching.

The fleet came closer, and Kenton watched the starmen scurry about their camp. They didn't know what to do—in ten years they had not seen so many aircraft together, and they were close to panic. But soon the fear passed. George passed the word around, and Kenton realized that everyone was too excited to ask him how he knew. George had told them the man who could remove the black mark was coming.

Soon the swarm of gyro-planes landed in the clearing, and the pilots came out. They stood in groups, uneasily, but one man walked boldly to the knot of starmen that had gathered about George and Brian O'Keef.

THE MAN WAS very big and very fat. Kenton had never seen such a fat man. The flesh hung from his jowls in great flabby chunks, and his round little eyes were deeply embedded. His clothing was beautifully tailored, but even so, his belly hung big and low over his belt.

George left the group and came over to him. "Mr. Atwell! You remember me, don't you, Mr. Atwell?"

Atwell considered, and the sweat clung to his face in big round beads. Then he nodded, and his loose jowls rolled up and down with the motion. "I remember you. I remember you vaguely. And I must apologize because I forget your name. But I met you on the outskirts of the city once. Now, as you can see, I'm ready to start things on a big scale. All ready. Everything's set now, and I've come into the hills for the starmen."

Brian O'Keef approached him and stuck out his big freckled hand. "Name's O'Keef. I'm sorta in command here. We work three years for you and then you remove the S? Is that the pitch?"

"That's the—uh—pitch. That's exactly what I offer. But let me tell you now, it will be hard work. Three years of hard work. There won't be an easy moment."

"We don't care. We don't care about that." The blue eyes sparkled under the flaming red hair. "What we want to do is get rid of the S. You can do that, and we'll work for you. When can we start?"

Atwell smiled and his small eyes were lost in the dosing pockets of flesh. "We'll start now. I have these aircraft here for you, and we'll leave at once. Is that agreeable?"

Captain Harkness came forward. "We're starting at once, you say? At once?"

Atwell nodded.

"Larkin, have you the orbit mapped?"

"Yes, sir."

"Kenton, you're ready at the controls?"

"I'm all set," Kenton told him. "You can relax now, sir." Then Kenton turned to O'Keef. "Brian, I'm telling you for the last time that this is a trick. George, here, is not a starman. Valerie has known him all her life and he is not a starman. Once you work for this man Atwell, he'll have you. You'll never get away, because he'll know who you are. Even if he removes the black *S*, he'll still know who you are. It's a trick, Brian."

BUT O'KEEF waved him away with an impatient gesture, and now the starmen were filing into the gyroplanes. Two at a time they filed in, and they held, their heads up and Kenton thought they could have been going back up the ramps to their starships.

Finally O'Keef said, "Well, Kenton, are you coming?"

"Of course I'm not coming! It's a trick. A low, stinking trick, and you're falling for it, Brian. Brian—"

"You're crazy, lad." And Brian had entered one of the airships.

George laughed in Kenton's face. George and a big giant of a man were alone with Kenton and Valerie now, and George laughed. "Well, Kenton, it looks as if you've lost."

There were tears in Valerie's eyes, but she smiled. "He hasn't lost, George. He hasn't lost. I'm still with Keith and we're together and you're the one who loses."

George flushed. The aircraft were taking off now, circling once, then heading away. Soon only one ship was left on the field. George stepped forward and slapped Valerie's face.

She fell back, raising a hand to her cheek, and Kenton sprang at George.

"You always want to be violent, Kenton," he said. Then he shrugged and crooked his finger at the giant waiting behind him.

The man lumbered forward. Valerie screamed. Kenton set himself and then swung his fists. He struck the giant full in the face, and he hit him hard, but the man shook the blows off like water. Then he clipped Kenton on the jaw with one huge hand, and Kenton felt himself falling. He tried to rise, but he could not, as he sank to his knees he saw Valerie striking at George's chest with her small hands, and he saw the giant lift her and tuck her under his arm like a doll.

The three of them reached the last airship. Kenton lay on his back, and everything began to reel. The clearing spun like a top, and the last thing he saw was the airship circling about above it.

CHAPTER FIVE
The Man in the Square

KENTON WAS stumbling back through the hills. He hardly remembered getting up, but he remembered the clearing, now empty, and he remembered calling Valerie's name, but he couldn't be sure because his voice sounded so strange there in the silence. His throat was dry and he had gone down to the spring and drank deep of its cool waters, and he was hungry, but he didn't stop for food. He had no time. He had to get back to the city on the hill. The fat man Atwell must have come from the city on the hill. Other cities were far away, and he must have come from the city on the hill.

It had taken Kenton and Valerie three days to get up and over the hills, but now in a day and a night Kenton was back at the starfield. He staggered to its edge and he wasn't surprised to find the ground car he had left at the foot of the hills. Few people came to the starfield.

He opened the door and climbed into the car and reached for the controls. His hands would not obey the orders of his brain. He slumped over the control panel and when he closed his eyes he saw Valerie's face and he thought he heard her scream.

He reached out but he could not touch her face and then he was sobbing her name and it mushroomed on his senses, driving everything else out. *Valerie...*

Kenton awoke with the sun in his eyes. He had reached the car at nightfall and now it was almost noon. He had not eaten in more than forty-eight hours and he was hungry.

He started the ground car and drove into the city. As long as he stayed in the car he was all right. No one would see the *S* on his forehead. The city hadn't changed. It was still small and crowded and at noon the throngs filled the streets. Kenton had a comparatively easy time driving because there were few cars. Not many people could afford them now.

Kenton found a cap in the car, a bright green plastic cap which he put on his head and pulled down low, and now he knew that unless one really looked for it, the *S* was invisible. He parked the car almost at the same spot where he had first taken it, and stepped out on the crowded street.

He saw the long line of weary people and learned that most of them were colonists. He stood at the end of the line as it moved slowly. When he reached the window a little old woman with gray hair handed him out a bowl of soup and a plastic spoon, and he ate eagerly. It was one of the synthetic grain soups and it tasted good to Kenton, warming him all the way down. Kenton returned his empty bowl and walked on down the street.

He didn't know where to go. That was the trouble. Although it wasn't a big city, it was a crowded one, and he didn't know where to look. Valerie might be anyplace here, a needle in a haystack...

Actually, he could not even be sure that Valerie was in the city on the hill. Atwell had a large fleet of aircraft, and they could have come from any place on the continent. Kenton did not want to think of this possibility. He had no means of transportation, and he did not want to think of it.

SUDDENLY, he was in the square. He had just gone on walking and his feet had taken him to the square. The first thing he noticed was that the statue was down. The great stone pedestal still stood and a little figure perched atop it, but the statue was gone.

And the square was crowded. He had been in the city many times and he had never seen the square this crowded before. The little figure atop the pedestal had the attention of the crowd. He was talking, but Kenton was still too far to hear the words. He did hear the angry restless buzzing of the crowd and he realized the people did not agree with the man on the pedestal.

There was something familiar about that figure, and Kenton came closer. Someone said: "What do you think of that, friend?"

Kenton said uneasily, "I don't know. I just arrived in the city and I don't know what's going on. Who is that man?"

"You got me there, friend. I saw the crowd and I came here to see what it was all about. I don't know who he is, and I don't like what he's saying. Something ought to be done about that. I think the guy's crazy. Listen."

Kenton listened. He still could not hear all the words, but he caught enough to know that the little man was talking about the starmen. He was saying that they were being unjustly persecuted, that they were the hope of the Earth, that everyone had degenerated but not the starmen, and that if Earth ever wanted to get back into space it had better realize which side its bread was buttered on.

Hoots came from the crowd. They were loud and it was an angry crowd and for a time Kenton could not hear the little man's voice. But there was something familiar about that bald-headed, bespectacled face. Kenton had seen it before. He tried to think where and for a time he couldn't. When he did, it was too late.

Someone climbed up on the pedestal behind the little man and grabbed him around the waist. The little figure struggled, but he was helpless in the arms of the giant who held him and soon his legs were kicking as he was lifted off the pedestal.

The crowd surged forward, and Kenton was swept along in the tide. He did not want to see what would happen to the little man and he knew he could not help him, but the pressure of the crowd carried him forward.

They were pushing the little man back and forth and his glasses had been lost in the scuffle. He was panting and his arms were two thin little flails trying futilely to protect him. He tried to talk, but he was panting so much that the words would not come out.

SOON THERE was no room to push the little man, and somebody held him and shook. Other people tore at his clothing and Kenton found himself yelling a protest, but no one could hear him. He pushed forward on his own now—he had seen enough. He did not know what help he could be, but he wasn't going to stand by and let them tear the little man to pieces because he had befriended the starmen.

And then Kenton knew. *Befriended the starmen!* He remembered that day in the square, weeks before, when the mild little man was with him when the kids were throwing stones. The mild little man who stood in the clutches of the crowd because he still spoke for the starmen. Kenton did not know who he was, in fact he did not really care.

He only knew that this was all wrong and that he could not let them do it and for one wild moment he forgot Valerie.

He tore into the crowd now, pulling them away from the little man, but no one bothered him. They simply thought he wanted to get closer himself so that he could go to work on the man who had no right to defend the hated starmen.

Kenton spun one man around roughly, and the big face glared at him. A blunt face, and Kenton recognized the man who had held him that day in the square. The man eyed him angrily, but Kenton still had on his cap and there was no recognition in the hateful eyes.

"Wait your turn, friend," said the blunt-faced man. "We all want to hit him. Just wait your turn."

Kenton could not do much against all those people, but he could steer the center of the mob away from the pedestal and toward one of the side streets. This was his plan and it was slow work. He saw the blood on the little man's face and the pathetic gestures of defense the small arms were making.

Now Kenton was directly behind the little figure and he grabbed him under the armpits and pushed. The mob wanted to follow, wanted to stay with the man and beat him, and gradually Kenton made his way to the side street. Once he almost fell under the rush of the crowd. But he knew that if he did he would never reach the little man again, and the small figure would be beaten to a pulp. Kenton held on grimly, and he pushed and occasionally he struck out with his hands. But no one noticed—it was a wild crowd and everyone was swinging his arms to hit someone if he could get them clear for a moment.

Kenton sensed there was something more to this. He was not merely saving the little man, he was saving more, much more. He did not know why he thought this, but the thought persisted. He was thinking of the little man as a symbol, and that might be the answer. Only that didn't explain anything. He knew that if he rescued the little man he also would rescue Valerie, that somehow their three destinies were interwoven, and that the fate of the starmen might hang in the balance too...

THE FRENZIED faces were leering at Kenton as he edged to the side of the square, and twice he had to reach out with one hand and push those faces away. He pushed the little man into one of the side streets and the crowd tried to swell through it after them. But the press was too great and only a few people got through. An arm reached out and the hand clutched at the little man, but it missed and struck Kenton high on the head instead. He felt the cap torn loose and he tried to reach up and grab it, but he was too late. Kenton's head was bared in the sunlight, and someone shouted in his ear:

"Starman! Starman! I'll be damned. It's a starman. No wonder he's helping the little guy."

There was a lot of noise and not many people heard him. Enough did, however, to make the situation a bad one for Kenton. Now the people who had pushed through to the side street with him were openly hostile, and Kenton found his way barred by a mob bent on stopping him and the old man.

Someone grabbed at Kenton's shoulder and wheeled him half about and a hard fist crashed against his temple. He felt his knees buckle. He did not know where the strength came from, but he picked up the little man and slung him across his shoulder, and then he ran. Feet pounded down the street behind him, and for a moment he was clear. Then faces appeared at the other end of the long, narrow alley and three men came plunging toward him.

They were less than a hundred feet ahead, and the mob was not half that distance behind him. On his left was a door, and, breathless now, he turned the knob and pushed. The door swung open and Kenton plunged inside with his burden. He dropped the old man down unceremoniously and he turned to the doorway. A man was halfway through it and Kenton lashed out with his leg and the man stumbled back, howling. Then Kenton slammed the door. It was a metal door with an old-fashioned bolt and he threw the bolt home. The fact that the door was of metal meant the house was one of the new ones which had been built hastily since the time of the Sanction, and what with the lawlessness in the streets, Kenton knew that the windows would be too high off the ground for anyone to reach them.

He ignored the pounding on the door and turned around. The little old man was staggering to his feet. Behind him Kenton saw a woman.

CHAPTER SIX
The Path to the Stars

SHE WASN'T very young, although Kenton decided that she once must have been pretty. Now there were lines in her face and her hair was partly gray. She seemed very surprised.

"What are you doing here?" she demanded.

Kenton smiled and said they were resting, and when the woman walked past him to the door he grabbed her arm and turned her around.

"Uh-uh," he said. "Definitely no. Stay away from that door and you won't get hurt."

"Just wait a minute," she snapped. "Who do you think you are? You come in here without knocking and now someone's pounding on the door—"

Suddenly she stopped. Her face turned white and Kenton let her arm go as she took a step away from him. She had seen the mark on his forehead. Kenton was smiling again. "Yes, I'm a starman. But don't worry, I don't bite and it isn't catching."

"Get out."

Kenton told her to sit down and she looked at him for a long moment, then moved over to a chair and made herself comfortable. Kenton began to walk around the room and the woman watched every move he made.

"Is there another way out of here?" Kenton asked.

"What do you mean, another way?"

"Another door. Anything. An exit."

"There's the roof. My husband is with the police and he has a gyro-plane, but it's not there now. When he comes back—"

"A gyro-plane, eh?" Kenton was thinking fast. He could still hear the crowd outside, but now the pounding had ceased. The voices carried and they were angry voices and he knew that soon they would bring a weapon and blast open the door.

"Anyone else in the house?" Kenton demanded.

"Um, no."

Someone yelled, "Mother. Hey, Ma—"

"No," said Kenton, smiling. "No one else is in the house."

"You leave my boy alone."

"Don't worry, lady. Not only don't we starmen eat people, we don't eat children either."

THE KID came in and he was about eight, short and too fat, with curly red hair and buck teeth. "Hey, Ma, I wanna—" And then he began to bawl. He had seen the little old man's beaten face and he saw the starman's mark on Kenton's forehead, and he began to bawl. He didn't stop, and it got on Kenton's nerves.

He shrugged and turned to the little old man. "You okay?"

"Well, I'm not exactly feeling chipper, young man, but I think I'll live—that is, if the mob doesn't get to me again. That's the trouble; it's been the trouble all the time. I really shouldn't, but I always want to make speeches. Say, don't I know you, young man?"

"We've met before. In the square, the day they were to take down the statue, remember?"

The old man said that he did and that he was glad to see Kenton again and that he had made up his mind about something. He was about to say what it was, but then they heard a faint droning, followed by a gentle thud on the roof.

"That would be your husband," Kenton told the woman.

She jumped out of her chair and before Kenton could stop her she was running up the stairs to the roof. Kenton sprang after her in time to see her legs disappearing above him through the trap door. When he pushed the door open, the man who faced him was holding a gun.

It was one of the emgee weapons that had been developed just before the Sanction, and Kenton knew it as a deadly thing.

"Okay, starman," the husband said. "Okay, just march right back down those stairs and relax. Come on, move."

Kenton turned slowly and started down the stairs, the man right behind him. This was his last chance, the last chance for everything, and the cold tube of an emgee gun was a foot from his head. He could hear the kid, still bawling downstairs, and from above, the woman climbing down behind her husband. She said, "I'm proud of you, Harold. Really proud. A trouble-making starman right in our own house, and you've captured him—"

Kenton stopped suddenly, crouching. The small of his back hit against the man's knees and the man yelled in alarm. Then Kenton lost his balance and the emgee gun went off and he felt the ray burn past his cheek. Something heavy came down on his back, and tumbling over and over, the man went plunging down the stairs. When he reached the bottom he lay still. Kenton called once to the little man and turned again to climb the stairs.

From above, the woman's foot kicked out and caught him high on his right cheek. Kenton stumbled and nearly fell. His head reeled, and it seemed there were three women above him on the stairs, all getting ready to kick again. Kenton grabbed the foot of the middle woman and then everything came into focus again. He held on to the foot and the woman screamed. She sat down and put her head in her hands and began to cry and Kenton didn't stop to quiet her.

He stood on the roof and soon the little old man appeared through the trap door and joined him. They ran to the gyro-plane and climbed in. At first Kenton had the same difficulty he had had with the ground car those weeks ago, but soon the aircraft rose up from the roof. Kenton looked down and saw the crowd hovering around the door of the house, and then he raised the craft higher and gunned it away from the city.

IT WAS night and the winds blew in from the north over the starfield. Kenton stood on the *Deneb's* ramp with the little old man. "You know, I don't even know who you are."

"I told you once I am a tourist. That's the truth."

"From where?"

"From—there." He pointed up into the sky.

"How can that be? You're an Earthman and there's the Sanction, so how can you be from space?"

"I assure you, I am. One thing you forget is the fact that ten years ago, before the Sanction, there were three billion colonists. Three billion.

"You starmen brought them back. Or, that is, you brought most of them back. But some really wanted to stay. Maybe they foresaw what conditions on Earth would be like when the population was doubled and the star-trade was ended, and they didn't want to go back. Not many, but some. Some hid out."

"So you—"

"Yes. I'm a colonist. There are several thousand of us, living mostly in the Antarian System. We've worked for ten years, *and we have tentative permission to take Earth back into space.*"

Kenton didn't say a word. He couldn't. He was suddenly choked up inside and no words would come out. Here was what he had been dreaming about for ten years; now it was a reality.

"I know what you're thinking," the little man said. "Well, don't be too hopeful. There are conditions. Any Earthmen I take out into space must be worthy of it. I'm the delegate. It's up to me. If I take the wrong ones and anything happens, we're through for all time. This the Interstellar Council swore. And all this rabble—they've degenerated in ten years. I can't take them. Who can I take up to the stars? Tell me that, who can I take?"

Kenton said, "You can take me. Me, Keith Kenton. You can take me. I'm a starman. You can take me and every other starman on Earth. Almost half a million of us. We could lead the way back to the stars for Earth."

"That's exactly what I've been thinking. I've felt it all along. It's the only hope. We can start with just one shipload. But we've got to work fast. Someone spotted me working on the *Deneb* recently—"

"Then it's the *Deneb* you'll take up?"

"Yes. I thought you knew. I came in a small ship, by myself, and it crashed near the ocean. I got out alive because it only was a slight crash, but my own ship is down on the beaches somewhere to the east.

"No matter, Kenton. The important thing is that we've got to go quickly. People have seen me tampering with the *Deneb*. It must have been a rare accident that brought them here, but they saw me. That doesn't give us much time. I've repaired the ship and it's just about ready for flight. Get those starmen and we will start—"

KENTON BEGAN to laugh. He sat down on the ramp of the *Deneb* and kept on laughing. The old man shook him by the shoulders, but he couldn't stop him. Kenton roared.

"What's so funny?"

"Nothing. Nothing's funny." Abruptly Kenton wasn't laughing anymore. "Nothing's funny at all. But I can't get any starmen. I can't get any starmen at all, and if people from the city saw you they'll be here before too long to see who's tampering with the *Deneb*. It's a taboo now; it's against the law. The police will be here."

"Why can't you get the starmen?" the little man protested. "In the city they tell me that the hills are filled with them."

"Not anymore. Not now. Somebody came along with a fantastic plan to get rid of the *S* brand on their foreheads in exchange for some kind of labor, and they all went with him. And they took my wife—Valerie."

Then Kenton told him the whole story, all of it. When he finished, the old man sat in silence, rubbing his cheek thoughtfully.

"Some kind of labor, you say?"

Kenton nodded.

"In the city?"

"I don't think so. I came back to the city because I had no place else to go, but I don't think it can be in the city.

Nearby, maybe, but not around here. The new influx of so much labor would be noticed."

The old man stood up. "Then let's go to sleep, Kenton. If we can get through the night without them finding us, we should be all right. No one will come out here at night; not with all the ghosts that ten years of superstition have created. And then tomorrow we'll find your starmen."

Kenton asked him how.

"Not now. Not now. I'll tell you tomorrow. I want some sleep, Kenton—and you can use it too. Let's turn in."

But Kenton did not sleep. He tossed restlessly inside the *Deneb* all night, waiting for the morning to come. After the first elation over the prospect of going back into space had passed, he felt depressed. They could go back into space, *if* they could find the starmen—and there was absolutely no clue as to where the starmen might be...

Kenton knew that he would never go back into space without taking Valerie with him. Valerie of Earth, Valerie who had never left Earth, and Kenton the starman. His hopes, his dreams, must wait until she was back in his arms...

THEY AWOKE early and breakfasted on food the old man had stored within the ship. Kenton didn't feel like eating, but he knew he needed it and he put away a good-sized breakfast. When they went outside, it was raining. The rain was coming down hard and the brisk wind swept it in sheets across the starfield.

Kenton said, "Okay, what now? You said last night you had an idea. Let's have it."

"Relax, Kenton. Take it easy. You're too jumpy, and you'll need your nerve today. We should be able to find your starmen, and from what you've told me, there may be trouble."

Kenton shrugged. "We'll get to that when we reach it. First we've got to find them."

"That won't be hard. You don't think they're in the city, because so much activity would be noticed. I agree. But you think they're nearby. Very well, we'll assume that, too. It makes good sense. Nearby, but not in the city—and we have a gyro-plane. We'll find them. We'll fly until we see the center of a lot of activity, and then we'll find them."

It was that simple. It was that simple, yet Kenton hadn't even thought of it. It might be just simple enough to work.

The rain felt good to Kenton. It seemed to be cleansing the air. Dripping wet, they plunged into the gyro-plane, and Kenton started the rotors. Soon they were in the air over the starfield, and, through the rain, everything below seemed gray and drab.

"It won't be easy to see anything," Kenton said.

"I know it. But the rain has an advantage, too. No one will be out to investigate the *Deneb* in this weather. It gives us another day, if we need it."

Kenton had an idea they would need it. Down below, he could see almost nothing through the rain.

It was mid-afternoon when the old man pointed toward the horizon with a finger that trembled. "See it, Kenton?"

Kenton looked. He squinted into the rain and the darkness. Off on the horizon, the broad circular area of light was the size of a one-credit coin.

"That would be it, Kenton. That would be it." The old man's voice was shaking.

They reached the area finally, and swooped low above it. There seemed to be no one out in the rain, but there were scores of tents and one long low building. And in the middle of the clearing, Kenton saw where the glow was coming from. It was a dull orange, almost yellow area—circular, about fifty feet across. Kenton scowled. "If I didn't know it was impossible, I'd say—"

"What would you say, Kenton?"

"I'd say that was the launching pit for an old-fashioned rocket ship. But that can't be. Rockets haven't been around for five hundred years, not after the space-drive and then the hyperdrive. So how could that be a launching pit?"

"I don't know how, Kenton—and I don't know why. Only that's what it is."

THEY BROUGHT the gyro-plane down and stepped out into the rain. There was no one in the clearing. It was a new camp; Kenton could tell by the freshly cut trees. But it was deserted, utterly deserted.

Kenton shrugged helplessly. They walked into the one building and found that it was a machine shop. Or it had been. Now it was stripped almost bare. At the rear they found a little office, but the only thing of interest there was a folder of bills. Kenton looked through it carefully and discovered that the material listed on them would be ideal for one of the old-type rocket-ships. Only it didn't make sense. That type of ship hadn't been used in over five-hundred years, and was so obsolete that it seemed incredible anyone would want to make one. Yet, outside, the slag still glowed in the blasting pit.

"I don't know," Kenton admitted. "I don't understand a thing."

The old man shrugged. "Look. It's a little late to tell you, I suppose, but my name is Wilton. It was Professor Wilton before I came on this mission to Earth. I was a professor of logic at the remaining Earth colony in the Antarian System. I've got a logical mind." He smiled. "At least I hope I have. So let's get organized in a logical way. Let's look at this thing clearly. Why would they build an old-type rocket ship, and where would they go in it?"

Kenton considered. "Well, they'd build an old-type rocket because they couldn't build a new space ship."

"Hardly," said Wilton. "You forget that there's a whole field of them near the city."

"Hmm. Well, if they didn't know how to operate the new type—?"

"Starmen? Ridiculous."

"I know. I know the answer now. They don't have fuel for a modern ship, so they had to build an old one."

"That's more like it." Wilton reached into his pocket and pulled out a little capsule. "Here's fuel for a space-drive and for a hyperdrive, in the new compact form. There's probably not another grain of it on Earth; it all was destroyed ten years ago. I brought this with me from the Antarian System, and it's much more than enough to get the *Deneb* back there. But without any of it, that whole starfield of ships is useless."

"Like the old ocean ships without an ocean."

Wilton laughed. "Hardly a good analogy, but you get the idea. Now then, that's why they built the ship. All right, for what purpose did they build it?"

"That," said Kenton, "beats the hell out of me. I don't know."

"Well, maybe *I* do. The Sanction cleared Earth out of space, you know. *But it didn't force us out of the Solar System.*

It never did that. And this man you mention—this man who promised to remove the black S for three years of labor—what sort of labor do you suppose he had in mind?"

"I don't know," Kenton said. "I don't know." They were on the track of something, and he knew it.

"Well, how about this? For ten years the human race has been Earthbound; and poor as hell. The standard of living has fallen through the floor. Not enough jobs, not enough mineral matter to keep things going—"

"Yeah!" Kenton roared. "I see it! This Atwell has an idea. A potent one, too. He'd go back into space, into the limited space we have, and start to carve an empire for himself of the mineral wealth in the Solar System. And all he'd need for that would be—an old-fashioned rocket-ship!"

"Precisely. And where would he go with his starmen laborers on the first trip?"

"Where? How should I know? The moon, Mars, Venus, the Jovian Satellites—how should I know?"

"He'd go to the moon. That's closest, and he'd go there because it would be as good a place to start as any. He'd go to the moon, and he's on his way there now. Even after the head start he's got, we could beat him in the *Deneb*. We could get there first. Which is exactly what we're going to do…"

CHAPTER SEVEN
The Firmament

THE BEAUTIFUL thing about these starships, Kenton thought, was the fact that they were almost automatic. You had to check the course and you had to check on little details. But when you were just hopping from one planet to another in the same System, it was a lark. The hyperdrive was different, of course. That was complicated, and you'd need a smoothly functioning crew to keep a ship going in hyper-space.

But now Kenton was ready in the *Deneb,* and he waited tensely beside Wilton as they prepared for the takeoff. It brought him back to a day, ten years ago, in the Fomalhaut System—and he began to tremble. He tried to brush the thought from his mind and he could not. But then he thought of Valerie, and he knew she was somewhere in space now, perhaps on her way to the moon in a new version of an antiquated rocket-and he forgot all about Fomalhaut.

"Ready?" Wilton demanded, and when Kenton nodded, the little man carefully emptied the contents of the small capsule into the tiny fuel chamber of the *Deneb.* The *Deneb* was a big ship, five hundred feet long and larger than any in the fleet except the *Arcturus,* Kenton knew, but that cylinder had enough fuel in it to take the ship to Antares and back. The old man had said so.

Wilton said, "What about the monitors, Kenton? Doesn't the Council have monitors?"

Kenton shook his head. "They do, but it won't bother us. We're allowed freedom inside the Solar System—out to a hundred million miles beyond Pluto's orbit, and about a fiftieth of a parsec 'north' and 'south' of the Solar equator."

"How did they figure on those distances?"

"That's easy. No captain would dare turn on the hyperdrive within that range, not if he cared what happened to the sun and the planets. And you can't go very far in one lifetime without the hyperdrive."

Then Kenton was busy at the controls, and the *Deneb* lifted gently from the starfield. It was hard to believe the ship held so much thunderous power within its walls. Kenton had always felt this way ten years ago and before, and he felt it now. The *Deneb* hovered above the field for a moment, a great metal dart there in the rain, and Kenton wondered if anyone from the city saw it. Then he opened up the space-drive and suddenly the view of the starfield and the city was gone.

Kenton leaned back and relaxed.

"We'll be on the moon in thirty minutes," he said. There was a tightness in his voice which he could not control. He was in space again. It was only a leap of a quarter of a million miles, a merest fraction of an inch by celestial reckoning, but he was in space again. He looked out at the stars—bright, steady pinpoints against a velvet background—something you never saw through Earth's obscuring atmosphere. And his thoughts were of Valerie…

HE PUT the *Deneb* down on a great flat expanse of pumice not far from Tycho's crater. And then the long watch began. The half-hour's flight was as nothing.

Looking back on it, Kenton hardly had been aware of the leap across space at all, but now he could see the huge crescent of Earth in the sky, pale blue and green and gray, and he kept his eyes at the scope. He wouldn't sleep until Wilton forced him away from the scope almost bodily, and then only when Wilton promised his own eyes would be glued to the instrument until Kenton awoke.

The moon was a wild dead place, but Kenton had seen too much of space to be thrilled by it. The fact that he had left Earth was exhilarating in itself, but without Valerie he knew he could not appreciate it.

It was Kenton who saw the rocket on the second day. It was a tiny black dot against the bright globe of Earth, invisible through the unaided eye. He shouted to Wilton, he pounded him until the little man woke, and then he cried: "See, Wilton? See? The ship! I'm not wrong, Wilton, am I? You see the ship, don't you? Look—"

Wordless, Wilton took the scope and peered within. He straightened and nodded his head. "It's the rocket, all right. How long, Kenton? When will it be here?"

"That's hard to say. About a day, I think. Twenty-four hours. Maybe sooner. I can't be certain."

Hours later, they could see the rocket easily without the scope, and soon after that the little black dot disappeared in the southern sky. Kenton took the *Deneb* up, and they could see the black dot to the south, breathing fire against the yellow pumice of the moon.

Then the rocket was down. Kenton saw the fire belch from its fore-tubes, and he saw it land.

"They'll get the surprise of their lives," Wilton said. "The last thing they will expect is another spaceship."

"Exactly what I figure, and the sooner we get there, the more surprise there'll be in our favor. I'll take the ship in, and you get a couple of spacesuits ready. You might check and see if there are any emgee guns in the supply room, too."

"I already have. There's a whole arsenal back there, Kenton. I'll be back in a moment."

The rocket had landed near one of the old abandoned Earth bases on the moon, and as Wilton returned, Kenton brought the *Deneb* down a few hundred yards away, on the other side of the silent dome. Men were back on a foreign world after ten years, and Kenton felt a sense of exhilaration.

He got into his spacesuit. After all these years, it felt cumbersome, but the emgee gun in his hands gave him confidence. He opened the airlock and moved along the narrow tunnel ahead of Wilton. A moment later the outer door swung in toward them, and Kenton stepped out onto the surface of the moon.

The mechanism of his spacesuit quickly adjusted gravity to Earth-norm, and he made his way around the edge of the glassite dome, Wilton following.

Ahead was the rocket, and Kenton began to run toward it. It was an incredibly small ship compared with the *Deneb*—not more than seventy-five feet long and half as wide, a bulky ponderous ship for its small size, resembling the pictures of Twenty-third Century rockets Kenton had seen.

They stood at the rocket's airlock door, waiting. Kenton leaned the fish-globe headpiece of his spacesuit against the hull of the ship, and presently he heard the hum of machinery which told him the lock was opening. He could feel his heart pounding, pounding so hard against his chest that it made him dizzy. The door swung in.

Kenton leaped in behind it.

THREE SPACE-SUITED figures stood in the narrow metal tunnel, staring open-mouthed at Kenton. Through the fishbowls he saw the three faces turn white, and then one of the men darted back and was pounding on the inner door. Kenton saw the outer door start to close, and Wilton got in just in time. Then the inner door swung open, and Kenton and Wilton followed the three men into the rocket.

With one hand he held the emgee gun on them, and with the other he took off his fishbowl. The air in the rocket was stale, but Kenton did not mind. Ten feet away stood Valerie.

She cried, "Keith! Oh, my darling!" Then she was in his arms and Kenton hoped Wilton would be holding the men off with his own emgee gun. But he didn't care. He could not feel Valerie's body against him through the bulk of his spacesuit, but her lips were soft on his, and that was enough.

George Bancroft had been one of the space-suited men, and the whiteness of his face remained under the Black S, but now it was the whiteness of rage. "Kenton," he growled. "Kenton..." The sound came out through clinched teeth.

Kenton herded them out of the rocket. He herded every last man out, and the very last was the huge figure of Atwell. His spacesuit was a special one—an ordinary suit would not have fitted his great bulk. He glowered at Kenton without speaking, but Kenton had never before seen such hatred in one pair of eyes—eyes small and almost hidden in folds of flesh.

It was easy. Kenton sensed that it was too easy. The starmen, of course, were happy after their initial shock, and flame-haired Brian O'Keef pounded Kenton on the back wildly after Wilton had told his story. "Back to space, lads," Brian kept mumbling. "Back to space…"

Kenton was too busy to listen. Jenkins and Larkin piloted the *Deneb* back to the star field near the city on the hill, and Valerie was in Kenton's arms all the way back to Earth.

THEY LANDED in the field with hardly a bump, and through the port Kenton could see the throngs of people outside. The *Deneb* had been missing from its place on the field, and the people had seen it returning.

Atwell snickered. "What now, Kenton? Go out there and they will kill you."

Kenton laughed. "Who's going out? I'm not. You and your men and George Bancroft are going out, but the rest of us remain. We're going into space."

Kenton had become careless. Half an hour ago, on the moon, there had been no resistance, and now he no longer held his emgee gun. Atwell reached into his jacket quickly, so quickly for all his size that Kenton could not stop him. When his hand reappeared it held an emgee gun. "That's where you're wrong, Kenton. March."

Atwell prodded him with the gun, and Kenton stood up. With Atwell closely behind him, he moved toward the air-lock. He heard Valerie call out, but he didn't turn to look back at her. He had been so near to everything he wanted—so near but not near enough. The taking of the *Deneb* was the violation of a taboo that he knew would bring the death sentence—if not legally, then at the hands of the crowd. Not for Atwell, no. Only for the starmen.

"Just you," Atwell purred. "You're the only one I want out there, Kenton. I'll need the rest of them back on the moon, after I convince the government how we can put the starmen to work for us in the Solar System to make Earth rich again. But not you, Kenton. You won't be there. You deserve something else. Now, march."

Kenton marched, and he was aware that George Bancroft was beside him, flanking his right side as Atwell flanked his left. George said, "You see, Kenton, you didn't get Valerie after all. She may not know it now, but she's mine."

Kenton struck out with his open hand and hit George very hard across the mouth. The blow jarred the big blond man, but before Kenton could follow up his advantage, Atwell clipped him across the base of his skull with the emgee gun, staggering him. Valerie ran to him, crying his name, but George pushed her violently away.

The airlock was open now, the ramp extended, and still there wasn't a sound from the crowd.

And then the sound came up in a mighty wave. "Starmen!" As one, the people surged forward. They had been on edge, Kenton realized, ever since the *Deneb* was gone—and now that it had returned and two out of three of the first men to emerge had the black *S* on their foreheads, that was too much.

The mob reached the foot of the ramp, and George, still smiling, pushed Kenton forward, saying, "Here's your starman. Take him." No one heard him, and he said it again, this time roaring the words above the growl of the crowd. "Take him!"

"*Starmen!*" It came again from the mob, and now a stone struck George's shoulder. He winced with pain and looked surprised. Then he understood and he put his hand to his forehead and screamed. "No!" he cried. "No, wait—"

More stones came, some of them striking Kenton. He staggered for a moment at the edge of the ramp before pulling himself back. Atwell had lost all control. The emgee gun was still in his hand, but it was meaningless. He stood there on the center of the ramp, and sweat oozing out in ugly beads on his face. Kenton shoved him and he fell and rolled down the ramp. Eager hands caught him at the bottom, and Kenton heard his screams above the noise of the crowd. The people from the city had seen the black *S* on Kenton's forehead and they saw one on George's, and they had assumed the *Deneb* was manned entirely by starmen.

Kenton turned and stumbled back up the ramp, a score of people clamoring at his heels. One reached out and Kenton heard an insane laugh. "I'm no starman!" The voice was sobbing through the laughter, and he knew it was George.

Eager hands helped Kenton back into the lock and slammed it shut. George was still outside, and through the port Kenton could see him clutching desperately with his fingers at the black *S;* the black *S* that would not come off his forehead. From somewhere inside the ship, a lever lifted the ramp and everyone outside rolled off. George was lost in the crowd as the *Deneb* rose up from the field.

THEY MADE one more stop on Earth. The *Deneb* was lowered again on the other side of the starfield, and Brian O'Keef forced all of Atwell's remaining men out. They didn't mind at all. They were only doing a job and they were paid for it, and now that their leader's plans had backfired, they wanted no part of the ship and its crew.

They were in space again. The starmen were singing, O'Keef and Larkin and Jenkins and Finer—the whole rollicking crew of them—a hundred men and a girl, blasting off for the stars again.

O'Keef's baritone was louder than the other voices, and Kenton could hardly hear Wilton as the little man spoke. "When we reach the range of the monitors, I will contact them. I am expected and we can get through. There will be a lot to do, Kenton. A lot to do."

"Yes," Kenton said.

"We must go out and show the galaxy that Earth is ready now. And in time we will return for the rest of the starmen. In time. In a century or two, perhaps Earth's billions can be taught to go into space again."

"Yes," Valerie said.

"Yes," Kenton said absently. "But it's a long way to Antares, too. A long way, and I hardly know my wife."

"Yes," said Valerie, and she took Kenton's hand and they walked down the companionway together...

THE END

If you've enjoyed this book, you will not want to miss these terrific titles...

ARMCHAIR SCI-FI & HORROR DOUBLE NOVELS, $12.95 each

D-131   **COSMIC KILL** by Robert Silverberg
  BEYOND THE END OF SPACE by John W. Campbell

D-132   **THE DARK OTHER** by Stanley Weinbaum)
  WITCH OF THE DEMON SEAS by Poul Anderson

D-133   **PLANET OF THE SMALL MEN** by Murray Leinster
  MASTERS OF SPACE by E. E. "Doc" Smith & E. Everett Evans

D-134   **BEFORE THE ASTEROIDS** by Harl Vincent
  SIXTH GLACIER, THE by Marius

D-135   **AFTER WORLD'S END** by Jack Williamson
  THE FLOATING ROBOT by David Wright O'Brien

D-136   **NINE WORLDS WEST** by Paul W. Fairman
  FRONTIERS BEYOND THE SUN by Rog Phillips

D-137   **THE COSMIC KINGS** by Edmond Hamilton
  LONE STAR PLANET by H. Beam Piper & John J. McGuire

D-138   **BEYOND THE DARKNESS** by S. J. Byrne
  THE FIRELESS AGE by David H. Keller, M. D.

D-139   **FLAME JEWEL OF THE ANCIENTS** by Edwin L. Graber
  THE PIRATE PLANET by Charles W. Diffin

D-140   **ADDRESS: CENTAURI** by F. L. Wallace
  IF THESE BE GODS by Algis Budrys

ARMCHAIR SCIENCE FICTION CLASSICS, $12.95 each

C-58   **THE WITCHING NIGHT**
  by Leslie Waller

C-59   **SEARCH THE SKY**
  by Frederick Pohl and C. M. Kornbluth

C-60   **INTRIGUE ON THE UPPER LEVEL**
  by Thomas Temple Hoyne

ARMCHAIR SCI-FI & HORROR GEMS SERIES, $12.95 each

G-15   **SCIENCE FICTION GEMS, Vol. Eight**
  Keith Laumer and others

G-16   **HORROR GEMS, Vol. Eight**
  Algernon Blackwood and others

If you've enjoyed this book, you will not want to miss these terrific titles…

ARMCHAIR SCI-FI & HORROR DOUBLE NOVELS, $12.95 each

D-141   **ALL HEROES ARE HATED** by Milton Lesser
AND THE STARS REMAIN by Bryan Berry

D-142   **LAST CALL FOR DOOMSDAY** by Edmond Hamilton
THE HUNTRESS OF AKKAN by Robert Moore Williams

D-143   **THE MOON PIRATES** by Neil R. Jones
CALLISTO AT WAR by Harl Vincent

D-144   **THUNDER IN THE DAWN** by Henry Kuttner
THE UNCANNY EXPERIMENTS OF DR. VARSAG by David V. Reed

D-145   **A PATTERN FOR MONSTERS** by Randall Garrett
STAR SURGEON by Alan E Nourse

D-146   **THE ATOM CURTAIN** by Nick Boddie Williams
WARLOCK OF SHARRADOR by Gardner F. Fox

D-147   **SECRET OF THE LOST PLANET** by David Wright O'Brien
TELEVISION HILL by George McLociard

D-148   **INTO THE GREEN PRISM** by A Hyatt Verrill
WANDERERS OF THE WOLF-MOON by Nelson S. Bond

D-149   **MINIONS OF THE TIGER** by Chester S. Geier
FOUNDING FATHER by J. F. Bone

D-150   **THE INVISIBLE MAN** by H. G. Wells
THE ISLAND OF DR. MOREAU by H. G. Wells

ARMCHAIR SCIENCE FICTION CLASSICS, $12.95 each

C-61   **THE SHAVER MYSTERY, Book Six**
by Richard. S. Shaver

C-62   **CADUCEUS WILD**
by Ward Moore & Robert Bradford

ARMCHAIR MYSTERY-CRIME DOUBLE NOVELS, $12.95 each

B-1   **THE DEADLY PICK-UP** by Milton Ozaki
KILLER TAKE ALL by James O. Causey

B-2   **THE VIOLENT ONES** by E. Howard Hunt
HIGH HEEL HOMICIDE by Frederick C. Davis

B-3   **FURY ON SUNDAY** by Richard Matheson
THE AGONY COLUMN by Earl Derr Biggers

WHAT WAS MAN'S TRUE DESTINY IN SPACE?

Bigwig News Chief Charles Wade had it on good authority that out near Titan, a little spaceman named Van Carlsberg had found a piece of the missing spaceship "Sunderling" floating in the void. The Sunderling had mysteriously disappeared in deep space several years earlier. But when Wade investigated he found that the little spaceman had been nowhere near Titan. So what was the truth of the matter? And more importantly, where did the fragment really come from? It could be the biggest story of the year, and Wade knew the answers might be found through use of the Martian Time Brain, an ancient mechanical portal into the past. However, no human had ever been allowed to use the Time Brain. But a back door deal between Wade and a member of the Martian Science Council soon had his ace newsman, Ken Waring, rocketing off to the red planet. What Waring found there was not only the truth about the Sunderling's fate, but the future of Earth's destiny in space.

CAST OF CHARACTERS

KEN WARING
This intrepid reporter had an assignment on Mars; but when he arrived on the red planet he got a story he couldn't believe.

CHARLES WADE
As head of Newscreen, his job was to get the good stories out to the public. But this story was going to be a hard sell!

YYRMAC
This blue Martian took a huge gamble when he concocted a plan to help his friend Wade. The only question was…would it work?

NNGAR
As one of Yyrmac's closest confidants, he was entrusted with a tremendous secret—something he wasn't thrilled about.

VAN CARLSBERG
He had been to Titan, found a piece of a missing spaceship, and returned to Earth—or so he thought.

THE TIME BRAIN
This Martian time portal had been a closely guarded secret for eons, but now it was at the disposal of a newsman from Earth!

AND THE STARS REMAIN

By
BRYAN BERRY

ARMCHAIR FICTION
PO Box 4369, Medford, Oregon 97504

CHAPTER ONE
Assignment to the Stars

THEY walked up the path from the garage together, scuffling their feet the way they always did.

"It was a good party."

She turned slightly, her hand on his arm. "Yes, it was. I wonder how the babes are."

He laughed. "Oh, they're all right. The new nursery glow-walls send them off to sleep in no time. The man who invented those things must have made his fortune. Do you know the glow dies down even if you're *pretending* to be asleep?"

"You and your science," she said, as she pressed her hand against the opener panel on the front door.

"We ought to get a vocal door operator, you know," he said, half to himself, as they went inside.

The bungalow was quiet and still, but in the lounge the visor screen flashed on and off—a number appearing and disappearing.

"Hello—the boss has been calling."

"What can he want, Ken?"

Her husband shrugged. "You ought to know—another job, I suppose. I'm not the star Newscreen reporter for nothing, you know." But it was odd. *Very odd.* Wade never called him at night when he had anyone else on hand, and there were plenty of others he could have got hold of tonight. The last time he had had a night call had been the night the Venusian experimental atom pile blew...

Jo stood in the doorway of the lounge watching the visor screen, her chin in her hand. "There's something..." she started, and then stopped. The still air of the room held the words that were not said.

"Darling Jo—what's the matter?" He watched her face working silently. They had been married long enough for him to know when she was going to cry. He turned away because he knew she did not want him to see. With his back to her he waited, then, at length, said, "Okay now?"

No answer.

He turned. "What is it, darling?"

"Just that something's wrong. He *never* calls you like this nowadays unless it's something big. Never. And I've felt something was wrong all evening. Something's happened or is going to happen. I *know.*"

He didn't laugh. "Go and take a look at the kids, Jo," he said. "I've got to get through to him."

She nodded and walked out of the room saying, "I know; this is just me being silly, I suppose."

He switched the visor on and asked for Wade's private number. The robot blonde smiled a metallic smile as she repeated the number. The screen blurred and then cleared. Charles Talbot Wade's florid face glared out at him.

"I pay you good money, Waring," his voice boomed out. "I pay you good money to be on tap when I need you. I've been trying to get you all evening. Where in heck have you been?"

"Sorry. I took Jo to a little party. We've only just come in. Just a few minutes back."

The face screwed up on the screen. A jaw like a shelf thrust itself into the Warings' lounge. "Well, don't stand there talking to me. You know I want you over here right away. Get yourself moving, man."

"I'm knocking on your door now."

The face smiled, a solid, generous smile. "Give my regards to Jo and tell her I'm sorry to have to drag you out."

The screen blanked out.

Jo came into the room with her husband's coat over her arm. "Here you are, darling. Try not to wake the kids when and if you get back."

Minutes later they stood in the hall together. The nursery door was open and they peeped inside. The glow-walls had died down long ago, and only the light from the hall enabled them to see the twin cots. He kissed his wife's forehead briefly. "I must go. He'll kill me if I'm more than five minutes getting over there."

"He won't and you know it. You're the best man he's got. Anyway, what sort of a job is it?"

"No idea. He sounded agitated, but then he always does."

Jo looked away quickly. "I know I can't stop you going, but I've just got one of my feelings. Something's going to happen."

He kissed her again, hard. *"Nothing's* going to happen. Now let me go. Go to bed, and stop worrying. I'll try and phone you if I'm not coming back tonight."

Then he was gone.

His beetlecar covered the distance from the bungalow to his office in a matter of minutes. The huge Newscreen House building stood, floodlit as usual, slightly off Fleet Street. In the square in front of it, the Screen itself, the biggest in London, was relaying visor pictures of an earthquake in Brazil, but at that hour of the morning there were only a few dozen people watching—all the night-haunters, thought Waring, as he stepped out of the beetlecar and raced up the steps of the main building.

The lift took him up to the third floor. Lights glowed from the boss's room. "Waring here," he announced at the voice box. The rose-glass door swung open.

"So you're here at last. If I'd known you were going to stop off for a meal I'd have sent someone to fetch you." The voice thundered in the cavernous room. Waring grinned and walked across to the circular desk where his boss sat, surrounded by visors, inter-office communicators, piles of paper, screwed-up cardboard coffee containers and all the other paraphernalia which made up his act as big-shot New-screen man.

"Well?" said Waring.

Wade heaved himself to his feet. He was a big man, well over six-foot and heavy into the bargain. His mouth pursed up before he spoke.

"There's someone in the next room I want you to meet. Van Carlsberg—you've heard of him?"

"The spaceman? Of course."

"Well, he's here. And I think he's got something that we can use. Something big."

There was a pause. Seldom had Waring heard his boss speak of a possible story as being "big." Generally it was "just another routine job—nothing to worry yourself about." And that applied to anything from a Martian troubadour's sudden death to a Venusian uprising.

"*How* big?" he asked.

"Possibly *very* big. Anyway—I've just had a long talk to him. I didn't have him in here when you came because I heard you say you'd been to a party and I wanted to see what sort of a state you were in. Whoever goes on this job will need a clear mind. How much have you drunk?"

"Hardly anything. It wasn't that sort of a party. And what does it matter how much I've drunk? It's an age-old law that a reporter works better when he's tight."

"Not on a job like this." Wade walked across to the adjoining room and opened the door. "Come on in," he said.

Van Carlsberg was a small man, with a leathery, puckered face. His hands shook continually and sometimes, too, his mouth would break into spasmodic twitchings. He was wearing a suit of dirty overalls, with the badge of space captain hanging by a few stray threads to the right breast pocket. Legend had it that this man had guided a rocket down through the Venusian clouds to land within a hundred yards of Venusport, after the automatic guide had failed and the astra-navigator passed out with fear. Legend had a lot of things, but this one was probably true. Waring held out his hand.

"Pleased to meet you. I've heard a lot about your exploits."

Wade's voice cut into the greeting. "I haven't told him anything yet. Sit yourselves down somewhere." He pressed a button and drinks swung out from the wall. "Help yourselves."

They poured drinks while Wade started to walk across the office. At the window he stopped.

"See up there? The stars. A long ways away, aren't they?"

Nobody answered.

"Yet somebody thought he could get there—remember? The first interstellar flight two years ago? Remember all the fuss when Henessey's superdrive ship left Earth—remember how all the paper's said they'd never come back and how Newscreen said they would?"

"Well?" said Waring.

"Well, they never did come back. The superdrive mathematics proved Einstein wrong about what happens when matter approaches the speed of light. Henessey proved by maths that a ship could travel *faster* than light and survive. Technically that first interstellar ship should have reached its objective. As you know, the Astronautical Association laid down that no further ships were to leave the system until something was proved about the success or failure of that first ship."

Waring grunted. "I know all this. Have you found out something about the ship?"

"Van Carlsberg has."

The little spaceman's hands shook as he lifted his drink to twitching lips. "That's right."

Wade turned from the window and glared at Waring. "Imagine the fantastic chances against ever finding anything of a ship that went right out of the system. Imagine the incredibility—the unbelievable luck; imagine all the million to one chances in the world. Everything was against anyone finding anything."

"Well, don't talk in riddles, tell me what you've discovered."

Van Carlsberg looked up. "My ship, *The Perroquet,* was returning from a trip to Titan. Our spotter screen picked up vibrations of something that wasn't a meteor. Naturally we investigated. It was part of a space ship hull."

Wade banged the table. "Tell me, Waring—what was the name of the first interstellar ship?"

"Why—er—the *Sunderling,* wasn't it? I think they named it after an old twentieth century naval vessel."

"Right. Now come downstairs."

The three men went out into the corridor and entered the lift. Outside the building a large beetle-van stood in shadow. Van Carlsberg opened the big double doors at the back and the three of them walked up the low steps inside. On the floor of the van lay a twisted, blackened hulk of metal.

They looked at it in silence.

From the metal there seemed to rise an odd, stale odor— the smell of time and space and destruction; an odor of other worlds. On it there were marks—deep marks as though some vast, gargantuan fingers had crushed what once had been a space ship as a child might crush a grape, letting this small piece fall away to circle endlessly in space.

"How can you tell this is from the *Sunderling?*" asked Waring.

His boss turned. "Have a look at the official records of ships that haven't returned. Find out how many of them were built up of this particular alloy metal. Check up on the parts that *were* found of the various ships and then add to the little pile of facts you get from those investigations—*this...*" He pointed.

Waring bent over the metal and looked.

"What is it?"

Van Carlsberg sucked in his breath with a dry, dusty sigh. "It's a groove in the metal, that's all. Just a groove. To anyone but a spaceman it wouldn't mean anything."

The reporter straightened up and looked from one to the other of his companions. He realized that they were both convinced that this piece of twisted metal was a fragment of the *Sunderling*. "What does the groove mean to you, then?"

"It means that the Martian magno-lock principle was used to bind the exterior plates together; and that's only been done on some six or seven ships altogether—one of them was the *Sunderling* and all the others are still space worthy."

"So?"

"So this is part of the *Sunderling.*"

They had proved it to him by deduction, but in fact he had known it from the start. The odor of space was about that piece of tangled metal, the odor of black midnights without end beyond all known planets. And the thought of the incredible luck that had brought this memento back into the Solar system rose up, engulfing every other thought.

"We'll go back to the office and talk this thing over," said Wade. And the spell was broken.

Back in the Newscreen office Wade paced up and down, speaking quickly, his sentences filling the room with a dry, ominous thunder. Van Carlsberg sat looking out of the window, and Waring, still trying to fathom what it was that Wade wanted of him, stood by the desk, listening.

"Imagine it, Waring—imagine the story behind it all—there must be a story, you know. The *Sunderling* had everything possible to keep it going steadily through space towards the stars—every gadget, every protective screen. It had the superdrive and four of the world's best brains on board. What happened? Why did it happen? Where? When? How? What makes a ship not come back from space? What happened to the *Sunderling?*"

Waring shrugged. "Well, there's no way of finding out." Wade stopped pacing. From outside came the brief sharp roar of the mail rocket blasting off for Mars. The sound came into the room from the silent night and Waring thought of another ship—a wonderful ship that set off for the stars two years before. A ship that never came back again.

The voice boomed. "There *is* a way."

"A *way?* A way to what? To find out?"

"Yes, a way to find out. A way to tell with absolute certainty what happened to the *Sunderling*. We've got what may be the greatest story of the year in our hands, Waring."

"But how?"

A silence came down like a great, still hand. It gripped the room and the three men for a moment and made them into statues, immobile. Then Wade spoke.

"Have you never heard of the Martian Time Brain?"

"Vaguely, yes."

"Well, that's our answer."

Van Carlsberg looked up, his face puckered like a wrinkled orange. "How much do you know about the Brain? I thought the Martians kept all their discoveries to themselves.

I've been on Mars a good many times and talked to quite a number of Martian scientists and they close up like clams whenever any of their pet discoveries are mentioned."

Wade nodded. "So they do; so they do. But I think I know one or two Martians who will help me and tell me anything I don't already know about the Brain."

The Time Brain. Waring had heard of it, of course. As a reporter he knew odd snippets about most of the new gadgets devised both on Earth and Mars. But the Brain was something much more than a gadget. It was a legend. He had heard reports of the way in which it worked, though he had no idea what the machine itself looked like. Apparently, it could be connected to any object, animate and inanimate alike, and could pick up the vibrations of that object in past time; that is, it could go back into the past and follow through the history of the object up to the present. Its findings were communicated to the enquirer by telepathic means. Waring had accepted the rumors as truth solely because the Martians were Martians, capable of making magic a scientific fact.

"You mean we should get hold of the Time Brain and find out about the *Sunderling* that way?" he asked.

"No, Waring. We shall take that piece of metal to the Time Brain. And you're going to take it."

"But for Heaven's sake—the Martian Science Council will never let us even *see* the Brain, much less use it."

"The Science Council won't even know we're there. I know Yyrmac, a politician who works with the Council. He's the chap who's been angling for free trade between Mars and Earth. He'll help. You can take a private rocket tonight. Yyrmac can meet you, smuggle you and the metal into the lab, and you need only be there a matter of days. Then you can take a rocket back and no one will know anything about it at all—until you get back here."

"But if the story's any good and you run it you'll have to disclose the fact that the Martian Brain was used to find out about it. You'll start an interplanetary war."

"We'll worry about that when it comes. Will you go—that's the chief thing at the moment."

"Yes, of course I'll go."

His boss smiled a long, spreading smile. Then his teeth came together with a sharp little sound like a twig snapping. "I thought you'd say that. There's a rocket waiting for you at the Newscreen field."

"What about Yyrmac?"

"He's already been told you're coming."

So it was all fixed. It was pleasant to think Wade had that much faith in him, but even so…

"Can I get through to my wife?"

"Sorry, old man. I'll get on to her tomorrow morning and tell her you're on a special job—covering this earthquake thing or some such story. You'd better not speak to her now."

Waring looked at the big man and nodded. "Can't trust me to talk to her, eh?"

"Let's just say that I daren't—in your own interests."

A small rain had started up outside and the windows of the office were stippled with the drops of it. Waring thought again of the twisted, blackened shape that lay in the beetlevan. He smelt again the smell of time and space and incredible distance that had clothed it. He shivered.

"What time does the rocket leave?" he asked.

CHAPTER TWO
The Time Brain

THEY brought the rocket down among the red Martian hills under the double Martian moons. They brought her down far from the towns and rested her on a bleak part of the planet where no one lived, where nothing stirred or had life of any kind.

Waring opened his eyes to the hard hand on his shoulder.

"What is it?"

"We're there."

"Mars?"

"Mars."

He stirred his legs and ran his tongue about inside his mouth. He had the hot, sticky fur of sleep still clinging there. He felt he wanted to vomit. "This is the right place?"

The spaceman beside him nodded. "This is where they told me to bring you. Right to this very spot."

"Is there anyone waiting for me?"

"I wouldn't know. All I was told was to drop you and blast off again. Ready to go?"

Waring nodded and looked across at the wooden crate resting beside his bunk. "Lucky they thought to put wheels on that thing."

They wheeled the crate to the port and lowered it down to the ground outside. "What's in it?" enquired the spaceman.

"Atom bombs," said Waring, sourly. "I'm going to blow Mars clean out of the cosmos."

The spaces man didn't even smile, but held the port open as Waring climbed down. "Luck," he called. Then the door banged shut and the seal cover crept down until Waring couldn't even tell where the door had been. Harnessing himself to the crate he pulled it down away from the rocket towards a small dip in the rocks.

There he crouched, sound flaps drawn up over his ears, hunched into the smallest ball he could make of himself.

Several hundred square feet of Mars shuddered; a million million Martian pebbles did a war dance among the rocks; a trillion trillion grains of Martian sand shifted and swirled, coiled and whirled and finally spiraled up to fill the space where just before a tall and stately rocket had glimmered and cast double shadows.

And Waring was left alone with a crate containing all that was left of the lost *Sunderling*.

He stood up and looked about him.

Mars.

He had been there before, of course, but always he had landed in one of the big space ports, where there were plenty of Earth people to welcome him. Out here it was different. Mars had been old when man's batrachian ancestors slobbered in their slimy lairs among the tree ferns of the Carboniferous age. It had been old then and it had been wise. Now it was just that much older and wiser. Waring felt the oldness and the wisdom of it. It was the same with the Martians, too. They gave you the feeling that somehow they knew something, something very important, perhaps more important than anything else in the whole Solar System.

He straightened his back and started looking about him. Wade had said that Yyrmac would meet him within minutes of his landing.

Above him the two moons stared implacably down, and beyond them the stars and all the mystery that they held. For the first time since the whole thing had started, Waring felt fear—an eldritch voice telling him to make for the town and get the next rocket back to Earth. He shook himself. The shakes, that's all it was. The Martian shakes. They said more people went mad on Mars than on any other planet. A tiny voice was saying, "Don't go on, don't go on…"

He kicked a pebble and started to walk about.

What could have happened to the *Sunderling?* Oh, yes, there were a million deaths in space to be had for the asking, but the *Sunderling* had a top rate spaceman and three of the best brains in the system aboard it. What was waiting up there?

The stars smiled a little, and did not reply.

Far away one of them did not smile a twinkling smile, but, instead, moved through the black midnight sky towards Waring. It came over the red hills which were red no longer, but dark, held in the hands of night; it came like a pale torch to settle not twenty yards from Waring as he stood with his feet apart, watching it.

The door of the hovercar opened, and a slim, blue Martian stepped out on four brittle, spidery legs.

"I am Yyrmac," said the Martian.

Waring strode forward. "Waring," he announced. "I was told you would be expecting me."

The Martian nodded. "Your employer has explained everything to me. It is in that crate?"

"Yes," answered Waring.

Yyrmac motioned to the Martian still inside the hovercar and from the nose of the plane emerged a blue snake that wavered and coiled and then settled on the crate. Half a hundred suction discs clamped firmly down; half a hundred steel and plastic muscles, galvanized into action by the tension of a million wire nerves, contracted. The crate was lifted like a child's toy brick and swung into the hovercar.

Yyrmac motioned again and Waring stepped up into the hovercar. "Is the Time Brain kept in one of the cities?" he asked as he watched the red mountains that were black with darkness slip by beneath.

Yyrmac shook his blue head. "When I heard from Wade I arranged with the Science Council to have the Brain taken to the Central Repair Laboratory for overhaul."

"Officially?"

"Of course. I know two of the chief members of the Council. They are aware of the advantages of free trade between Mars and Earth. I told them that I needed the Brain to do a specific job for an Earthman friend, who, in return, would help in the drive for free trade. Wade is a very powerful man in political circles, as you know. I think with his help we may win your Government round."

Waring nodded quickly. "Yes, but the actual removal of the Brain—I mean are we officially going to use it? If so, why all the secrecy'!"

Yyrmac rolled liquescent silver eyes. "The Science Council is not the same thing as the Government of Mars. I am a politician and I am well aware that the Science Council does many things of which the Government is unaware. Sometimes it is best for a politician to close his eyes."

Waring looked puzzled. "You mean you are helping us because you want us to help you in return?"

"Partly that. Also I am idealist enough to believe that knowledge should never be withheld. You wish to find out what became of your interstellar ship. The Time Brain will tell you. The Martian Government might deny you the means of finding out. The Science Council would not."

Waring laughed. "Your system is almost as bad as that on Earth."

Yyrmac gazed out of the port so that Waring could not see his face. "Sometimes, though, I think scientists are too generous in the amount of knowledge they give away. Sometimes it is perhaps better that people do not know…"

"'Do not know *what?*"

"What a beautiful night it is," said Yyrmac, just as though he had not heard.

Below them, through the ports, they could see the silver lanes of the canals, and beside them, nestling like crabs along a submerged seawall the buildings of the towns. Suddenly the hovercar changed course and headed once more towards the high land, leaving the glitter of the lights and the gleaming streak of the canal behind, plunging again into blackness.

Waring felt the antiquity of the planet, even though he was speeding through the night in an up-to-date hovercar. On Mars it was always antiquity that you felt, no matter whether you were treading the red deserts or wandering the streets of the white little towns; no matter when or where or what, it was always the antiquity. You might be sitting in a Martian Government office amidst their most modern scriber machines and vision sets. You might be wandering in the incredible cities of Kotharuum, with their fairytale columns and pinnacles; anywhere at all you might be, and you would feel the age of Mars all about you, rising like a fragrance from every little thing.

The hovercar started downwards towards a circular, rocky basin, Waring could not see any buildings, but he felt that the journey was over, somehow.

The journey was over.

The hovercar settled itself like a giant bee on a square of concrete. The two Martians followed Waring out.

"You said we were going to the Repair Laboratory—is this it?" queried Waring. The Martian Yyrmac nodded his long, blue head.

"It is. The laboratory itself is to our right."

"Then why can't I see it?"

Yyrmac laughed. "Have you never heard of the famous and highly secret Martian tape mentalfilms? We use them on all buildings of this kind for camouflage purposes. The business was started when there was threat of war with Earth ten years back. The scientists working out here got so used to them that they were never taken down. You are scarcely twenty feet from the front of the laboratory at this moment. The mentalfilms take your thought patterns, record them, and relay them cinematically on plastiscreens. Thus you see only what you expect to see—that is bare rock."

"But surely the cost of having these things here when they are no longer needed—"

"The cost of plastiscreens and mental films is very much less than the cost of new scientists. Apparently when the threat of war was over the films were abandoned, but the scientists had become so used to seeing what they *expected* to see that the sight of what was really there upset them. Four threatened to resign—one *did* resign. It was all rather amusing."

Yyrmac said something in Martian and the bare solid Martian rock that Waring had been examining shifted in some obscure fashion. An angle formed where an angle hadn't been, and there, quite suddenly, was a door.

Yyrmac smiled a blue smile. "Shall we go in?"

Inside there were other Martians, one of whom came across the shimmering hallway to greet them.

"Ah—Yyrmac. We heard you were coming. This is Mr. Waring?"

Waring nodded, feeling ill at ease here, with so many Martians and no Earthmen. Luckily many Martians had learned English, and, indeed, most of the Earth languages. It seemed they could study language and learn it all within the ticking away of a few Martian seconds. Waring often wondered whether they did it by telepathic means. No one knew. There was no way of finding out, either. Ask a Martian how he knew your language and he would smile one of those enigmatic smiles and roll his liquid eyes at you as though thinking: "How stupid these Earthmen are, *really*, how stupid—"

The Martians were talking in their own tongue now, and Waring took the opportunity to look about him. They were in the hallway of an enormous building, pillars of glittering metal held up a crystal roof. Rooms led off in every direction and spidery blue Martians came and went on spidery blue legs. Through the whole building there came a humming and a buzzing, presumably from the generators necessary for the repair work. Waring found that both the Martians had stopped speaking and were looking at him.

"Shall we go on?" said Yyrmac.

"Of course."

They walked down crystal corridors and the Martians' brittle legs made strange, crackling, rustling sounds as they walked.

Waring found that he was wondering whether Yyrmac was really on his side, whether this were not all a great trap, whether this and whether that.

The rustlings of the Martians' blue spidery legs filled the corridor.

At last they entered the room where the Time Brain was kept. Waring had never seen it before, had never seen pictures, visionplates or anything, yet he knew it was the Brain.

It sat roundly on a slab against a wall, sleeping. It was a bright, burning egg squatting in a nest of wires and insulators and resistances and steel rods and tubes and discs. It was a sleeping Martian God. On the right of it there was a black metal chair, about which coils of wire and metal discs and more rods and tubes jutted in complexities. On the left two multi-jointed metal arms, with suction attachments, lolled to the floor. It was a God, that's what it was, thought Waring; it was the all-seeing eye of the ancients, squatting there like a billious metallic idol. Only a Martian would have made it so complicated. He walked over and stood looking down at it with a frown on his face.

"What *is* it, really? How does it work? Who invented it?"

"You came to use it, not to ask questions about it."

"That's all very well, but—"

"I'm afraid we can tell you nothing, Waring," Yyrmac went on. "While I can let you *use* the Time Brain, there is no Martian alive who will tell you anything about its construction. Eventually I have no doubt that your own scientists will discover the principle involved and somebody else, like your employer, will see the commercial possibilities of the Time Brain principle and you will have them all over your planet."

"Commercial possibilities?"

"Of course. I should have thought that as an Earthman you would have recognized them immediately. Imagine—for a fabulous fee, payable in advance, you could take a year's holiday through the ages all within the space of a few hours or perhaps days. The Brain could be connected up with something very ancient and there is your holiday for you. A piece of one of your ancient sailing vessels enables you to take a holiday with an ancient sea captain of another age and so on and so forth."

Waring laughed politely.

"Do you wish to start now?" asked Yyrmac.

Obviously they wanted to get rid of him, thought Waring. "Yes, I suppose we might just as well." A hot, sticky fear crept up from under his suit and started tightening his throat, started crawling about his neck like a warm snail, slowly. Now he was going to find out what happened to the *Sunderling;* he was going up, up, up to the blacknesses and the depths, up to the outer reaches of space with three men who were now no more than dust blowing through the cosmos. He saw two Martians wheeling the crate into the laboratory.

There was a crackling, as the wood was torn open. From the roof a suction arm snaked towards the relic of the *Sunderling*, coiled, descended.

"Sit in the chair, please."

Like a dentist's, thought Waring; just like a dentist's. There came again that hot fear and then a coldness settled on him. The humming of the generators sounded dully. A dentist's drill...

"The arms, as you see, are connected to the object," said Yyrmac. Waring watched the suction arm bring the metal fragment over to the Brain, where the other Martians connected the jointed metal arms to it. Plugs were plugged in, wires were examined. Round the Brain the Martians rustled on fragile legs, examining this, connecting that.

A helmet, fitted with circular pads, was lifted and fitted over his head. This was joined to the Brain by a tube. Busy, brittle Martian fingers adjusted, fiddled, altered.

Why had the Martians themselves never tried space travel beyond the Solar System, thought Waring, sitting there in a black metal chair, with a curious helmet on his head. Why, with all their science, all their ability, had they never dared interstellar flight'?

The whine and hum of the generators mounted. A green night beetle flew lazily across the great room. The Martians stood back. And the antiquity of Mars, the age-old knowledge and serenity was even there, in the most modern laboratory on the planet, in amongst glass and crystal tubes and insulators and resistances and wires and coils and glass floors and the humming and whining of modern machines. Yes, the antiquity was there, too.

And suddenly the antiquity and the knowledge were not serene and placid things anymore. Suddenly Waring felt afraid of the Martians who stood there. And he could not think of a single reason why he should. No, not a single reason.

Yyrmac cleared his throat, raspingly. "I have set the Brain so that you will arrive on the ship shortly after it left your planet. I imagine you wanted that."

"That's right."

"You will understand that while you will *live* the experiences of the crew of that ship you will not be anyone of them; you will be an observer, able to pick up the thought patterns of each or any of them. Also while the experiences may seem to you to take days, weeks, months, *years* even, they will all be over in a much shorter period, according to our own measurement of time."

Waring tried to nod his head, but the helmet prevented him from doing so. What if I'm killed in the past, he thought, will I ever come back here? Will I get back to Earth, to Jo and the kids? He remembered the way she had looked at him on the evening that Wade's call had come through. She had known something was going to happen. The humming of the generators made his thoughts into a swarm of angry bees. What made the Martians so complacent about all this? Why had they never been into outer space themselves? They had spaceships and there were rumors that the Henessey superdrive was merely a development of a Martian concept known and used when men were still running about with wode on their faces. If that was so, why had the Martians never used it? Why? Why?

The helmet pressed into his head. He ran a thick tongue round his mouth. "Well?" he said.

Yyrmac smiled at him, sadly, Waring thought. "Now?"

"Yes, now."

There was a rustle of legs. Needle fingers pulled two flaps down from the top of his helmet over his eyes. He heard a series of clicking sounds and the generators increased their noise. He was in darkness. Desperately he tried to direct his wandering thoughts away from the fear that he felt. Images of Jo and his children fluttered like angry moths in front of him. Then it was Wade in his office saying, "What makes a ship not come back from space? What happened to the *Sunderling?*"

And then the darkness became a redness and a fire and the noise of the generators became a vast and terrible music and all the images went scuttering off into the dark night of what is now, while Waring swept back, ever back, to what had been.

The Time Brain throbbed and pulsated. It changed from blue to pink and deepened to a rich red. The hum of the generators rose to a screaming and Yyrmac smiled.

The other Martian turned. "Why did you let him'?"

"It had to come some time."

"But why now'?"

"It is to our advantage to please this man Wade. He can help us more than you think. On Earth he is a very important figure in politics."

The other Martian rustled his legs impatiently. "Yes, yes, I know. But *this!*"

"We shall, at any rate, find out just how adult this Earthman is."

"But do you think the others are *ready* to know yet?"

Again Yyrmac smiled. "I don't know," he said. "I just don't know."

They watched the Time Brain shimmer, glisten, radiate.

Ten thousand star shells burst about Waring's head and he was lifted out of the chair and thrown up to a great height into a ruby void far beyond Mars, far, far...

It was as though he was looking down on himself, suddenly. He had split up into two parts, one of the parts was left there sitting in a black metal chair and the other part soared away and beyond everything, soared up into purple vastnesses and black midnights where time had shrugged its shoulders and given up for lost and where space was as big as eternity and was only, even so, just one of the millions of spaces that there were.

A cloud floated by the part of him that was in space. Then it was not a cloud, but Yyrmac's blue, crinkled face. And Yyrmac was speaking. "You will understand that while you will live the experiences of the crew of that ship you will not be anyone of them; you will be an observer, able to pick up the thought patterns of each or any of them." The cloud grew larger, larger. Then it wasn't Yyrmac anymore. It was Jo, and she was standing in the lounge with her hand on the door lintel, saying, "He *never* calls you like this nowadays unless it's something big. Never. And I've felt something was wrong all evening. Something's happened or is going to happen. *I know.*"

Then the cloud became the vast egg of the Time Brain, floating among a million slurs. But the Time Brain was a face, too. A huge, florid face framed against a giant window.

Wade: "Imagine the story behind it all—there must be a story, you know. The *Sunderling* had everything possible to keep it going steadily through space towards the stars; every gadget, every protective screen. It had the superdrive..."

Yet the superdrive was supposed to be a development of an ancient Martian theory. Why had the Martians never tried to get to the stars? Or had they tried? If they had, what had happened?

Star shells again burst about him. A leprous moon scudded past, leering. The distant noise of the generators became a great booming of organ music, echoing and re-echoing in a terrible symphony. And the star shells were suddenly not star shells any more but real stars, floating by him as he sped outwards to the ultimate ends of the universe.

And another part of Waring sat in the Martian Repair Laboratory with a strange helmet on his head. But memory of that other part was fast fading from the mind of the Waring in space.

Then the blackness and the redness came up again to smother the images, cover up the visions. It swirled up from where the star shells had been bursting, swirled like a hideous polypous mist. The sensation of soaring through space disappeared and Waring found he was falling, slowly, slowly, as in a dream. He could see nothing but the blackness and the very dark redness all about him and so he could not tell whether or not he was really falling or whether it was all imagination. Then the blackness closed in, pressing on his eyes; it sent exploring dark hands into his ears, his nose, his mouth; it caught on his throat and *twisted*...

Momentarily Waring found the blackness vanish. In its place there was a *different* blackness. The simple blackness that he knew well—that of ordinary space. Stars glittered as he had seen them glitter before, through the window of a ship speeding out from Earth towards another planet. He was not in a ship now, however, but standing on a black, rocky plane, whose dimensions were oddly *tangled*. Near was far, and far was piling up on top of him. He ran a hot hand over his face and looked again. Something was moving there on the plane, something shadowy and unreal, a ghost figure moving like a wisp of dust across a nightland of his own imagining. And he knew that whatever it was he was looking at was something to fear, something alien. Nearer it came, slowly moving on the blackness of the plane. And somehow Waring could get no idea of what it was or how big it was. Then the stars welded all together into a solid ball of light and flew down from their heights to swarm round his head. Then the blackness came again and the vision was no more.

"What do you think will happen when he finds out?" asked the Martian.

Yyrmac shrugged. "I've no idea," he said.

"But surely you must have thought about it?"

"Perhaps I have."

"Well, then?"

"Really, you know, I've simply no idea what will happen. Presumably it will be up to Wade."

"Do you think our government would have agreed to let the Earthmen use the Time Brain if they had known what they were going to try and find out? Do you for one moment imagine they would?"

Yyrmac did not answer for a moment. Then he said, "I suppose not, but anyway I rather doubt whether Wade will say anything to anyone when Waring tells him what he finds out."

The other Martian scuffed brittle legs. "Why not?"

"Earthmen are not Martians, that's why not. They are a young, hysterical race, with nervous temperaments. If the discoveries that Waring makes are made known to the Earthmen through Wade's Newscreens there is every possibility that they will not be able to stand the strain—if, that is, they believe them at all. As I say, I do not think Wade will even attempt to make these things public."

The other Martian shrugged.

The generators hummed their melancholy hum.

The Time Brain pulsated redly against the wall.

CHAPTER THREE
Black Hand of Space

THE ship was moving with incredible speed. It was saw-ing space into a million dusty pieces as it moved in the darkness.

Waring was aware of all this. He did not know exactly *how* he was aware of it, but he was. He was in the ship and yet he was not in it; could touch things, yet could not touch things. At first he had been a part of the ship itself and had been roaring through midnight darkness with stars and meteors and emptiness below him. Then he had found that he could move. And he had moved—through the ship. Now here he was in a giant control room among panels and dials and glowing screens. It was the *Sunderling*.

Voices seemed at first to be distant, far away. Then he realized that it was merely that the noise of the drive tubes and motors was drowning them.

When the *Sunderling* had first set off, most people, scien-tists and laymen alike, had declared that Henessey's theories were crazily impractical and that any ship that relied on the new superdrive would meet failure. Only a small knot of revolutionary thinkers had thought that Henessey was right. Waring vaguely remembered Henessey's articles in the *Astro-nautical Journal* describing some of the principles involved in the superdrive that involved the use of Martian Fyyric mathematics, which were generally believed to be beyond any Earthman's comprehension. It was then that rumors had started regarding Henessey's debt to ancient Martian science. A debt that he was too egotistical to acknowledge.

Now here *he* was. Kenneth Waring, Newscreen reporter (or part of him, anyway), floating wraithlike in the first interstellar ship that had been destroyed years before. He felt his thoughts trailing off and it occurred to him then that this was the end of the transition period. He was growing to be no longer Kenneth Waring or aware of what Kenneth Waring thought or felt; he was growing to be a reception visor, no more than that. A mechanical instrument designed to assimilate and record, assimilate and record...

Henessey fussed like a bumblebee on a rose; his white hands fluttered like butterflies as he examined the dials. On a hammock McOrdle slept. Rumbold played chess with the electronic player. Nolan stared at the spotter screen, watching the stars, impassive.

Just the four of them there were. Just the four. And they were all of them waiting for Henessey to put the superdrive into action, fearing what would happen when he did. Up to then the ship had been motivated by the normal reaction jets and they knew that soon the superdrive would be cut in.

Rumbold lit a cigarette. "This chess player is remarkable, you know," he said.

"Remarkable? Nonsense."

"I don't mean remarkable for being able to play chess; I mean remarkable for being inconsistent in its moves. It plays to no pattern."

Henessey turned crossly. "Of course it isn't consistent. If it were consistent any intelligent creature could beat it, after learning the successive moves it made."

Rumbold shrugged. "I know. I was only trying to make conversation."

From his seat Nolan laughed. "Unused to space, Rumbold?"

"Unused to *this* sort of space."

"By and by you'll get used to it."

"I don't mean just interstellar space."

"What do you mean, then?"

"Don't *you* feel it?"

Henessey looked up from his control dials. "Feel what?"

Rumbold got up and moved across the cabin, his eyes blinked wildly. "Feel what it is, that's all. Just whatever it is."

Clack went a spanner in Henessey's hands. "What *are* you talking about, Rumbold?"

"I don't know. I don't know. Only that something's wrong. I can feel it. Something trying to *push* against my mind."

From the hammock came a stirring. McOrdle's voice rasped out, "I've had that feeling for the past twenty minutes."

The four men looked at each other. McOrdle propped up in the hammock on his elbows, his eyes owlishly staring.

"Well, it's all imagination," snapped Henessey. "This is no time to get nerves. The superdrive cuts in in fifteen minutes, so you'd better get prepared."

Rumbold walked over to the spotter screen and looked at the pinprick stars. He lit another cigarette.

"Look at them. Just *look*. Can you wonder we feel queer?"

Henessey's voice came tightly. "Remember only two of you feel queer. *I* am having no hallucinations, Rumbold."

"I am," said Nolan, softly.

Henessey rounded on him. "I thought you were supposed to be a spaceman, Nolan. When I hired you it was because they said you had iron nerves and knew just about all of space there was to know."

Nolan shrugged. "You get used to space; you get to know it, perhaps too well. It gets to be no different from anywhere else after a while; it gets friendly towards you and you feel at home in it. So naturally you know it when something's wrong with it."

"Wrong? Wrong? What are you talking about? Nothing's wrong. We've had a few minor mishaps, certainly, but they were to be expected. I never thought I should hear you saying things like this, Nolan. Rumbold, yes. He hasn't been up in space much before."

"Don't be personal," said Rumbold, sourly. Then, turning to Nolan, he said, "What's your theory?"

"I don't know. There are still a lot of things about space we have never found out. Maybe this is one of them. But it feels as though, as you said, something's pushing against me—a sort of psychic force."

"And you're a spaceman!" sneered Henessey.

"I'm not such a damned fool as to imagine that we know everything there is to know about the universe, if that's what you mean."

"That is not what I mean, and you know it."

There was silence in the great black ship, save for the roar of the drives and the motors and the clicking of instruments. And the ship sped on through space.

Minutes passed with still no one speaking. Then Henessey said, "McOrdle—take a look at this."

McOrdle swung his slight body off the hammock and shuffled across.

"Look at what?"

"This dial."

McOrdle looked and breathed out in a deep sigh. "It must be the generators."

"Nonsense. The generator room is webbed with beams. If anything had gone wrong down there we should have had alarm bells ringing instantly."

"Well, there might be something wrong that the beams missed."

"I doubt it."

"If not that—then what?"

"That's what I'm asking you; you're the engineer."

"I'll take a look." He turned and walked to the hatch. Beyond the control cabin the artificial gravity did not function, and, standing by the hatch he turned, saying, "If you hear anything floating about down there it's only me." Then he went down.

Rumbold strolled lazily over to where Henessey was fussing with the dials, his hands busy again, fluttering.

"What's up?" said Henessey.

"Dial not registering properly."

"What's wrong with it?"

"Don't know. McOrdle's gone down to look at the generators. Hey, look at *that*, too."

Rumbold looked.

"Another dial fading out."

Rumbold nodded. "Something's sapping the power."

"But it can't be. Here, Nolan. See what you can make of it."

Nolan joined the others, peering at the dials.

"Here's another, look. Speed regulator this time—yet if we'd slowed down in any way we should have noticed the change in the jets."

A silence came down over them, and each felt the dread of something unknown, unplanned for.

"I don't like it. I don't like it at all," said Rumbold.

The spotter screen showed them a trail of meteors blazing past; dragon's eyes in the night of space.

"I hesitate to use the superdrive until we find out what's wrong here," said Henessey, somewhat shakily.

"Nothing's wrong here," said Rumbold.

"What do you mean, nothing?"

"Just that. It isn't here that anything's wrong. It's out there," and he pointed at the screen, where an inky depth was pitted with stars.

"Stop being an imaginative fool. Whatever is waiting for us, if we ever find a habitable planet, is still a good many light years away."

McOrdle's head came up from the hatch. "There's nothing wrong down there that I can see," he said. And then he watched the three men with a puzzled look. "What's up now?"

"More dials not functioning properly."

"Oh, why did I leave Mother Earth?" said McOrdle, and then he came across to join them.

"You're sure you checked on everything?"

"I checked everything the beams might have missed and a few that they couldn't have missed. I also checked on the beams themselves. They're in perfect order."

Nolan was stroking his jaw with a lean, burned finger. "Did any of you notice something else?" he said.

Nobody said anything. Nobody moved.

"What?" said Henessey, then.

"It's getting darker in here."

"Imagination."

"I tell you it's getting darker. Look at the lights."

They looked. Four pairs of eyes staring steadily at the bars of light that ranged the cabin.

"He's right," said McOrdle, presently.

The lights were dying slightly within themselves; slightly, slightly. But they were dying just the same.

"McOrdle, take a look at the lights," said Henessey.

So McOrdle took a look at the lights.

"Nothing wrong. Not a thing."

After that they just stood and looked at things; at the dials on the control panels, at the lights on the walls, at the big suspension capsules waiting for them when they cut in the superdrive. At everything they looked, each knowing that something was very wrong with the *Sunderling*.

"Well, we can't go back now," said McOrdle, smiling a little.

"Like a dream," said Rumbold, under his breath.

There was a tenseness. "What dream, Rumbold?" said Nolan.

Rumbold looked at the spotter screen, saying, "Oh—I didn't specify any special dream, did I?"

"Perhaps you didn't. But did you *mean* a special dream?"

Rumbold looked across at the spaceman. "Did you dream it as well, then?"

Nolan nodded.

"How about you, McOrdle? Did you have a strange dream last night?"

McOrdle nodded.

"Well, I had a strange dream, too," shouted Henessey. "What has that to do with our instruments getting the willies?"

Rumbold shrugged. "It may have nothing to do with it at all. The point is that we all had strange dreams. I noticed strained faces and odd looks this morning. Your remarks have confirmed them. My own dream was a definite warning. Were yours?"

"Yes," came from three hoarse throats.

Rumbold nodded. "Collective hallucinatory dreams."

"But why?" asked Nolan.

"That's what I don't know. It seems either that we were all in some way aware that we were going to run into trouble somewhere and the dreams were the stronger subconscious protective instincts coming into play, or else..."

"Or else what?"

"Or else the dreams were deliberately put into our minds."

Henessey laughed. "Oh, Heaven protect me. I never thought I should hear a psychologist talking like a lunatic." He shut his mouth with a crack of teeth. "Listen, man. We are on a very advanced type of spaceship in a very advanced age. We are all intelligent men. To hear you talk one would think we were off to the Salem witch trials or some such thing."

The lights dimmed further.

Dials flickered; needles hovered and did things that needles shouldn't do within the dials.

A strange, tense feeling of darkness came into the cabin. It wasn't just the dimming lights. No, it was more than that.

"Anyway, we can't waste time over dreams," said Henessey, fussily. "If something's tapping our power, then it's something organic. Nothing in the psychic plane can dim a light."

"What are you going to do?" asked Nolan.

"I'm going to step up the power. If the lights are dimming a step up should bring them back to normal. Then we shall see what happens." He pulled a lever, flicked a switch.

A humming crept up to a slight screaming. The lights still dimmed. Sweat started to form on Henessey's face. "It is the power," he muttered to the control panel, to the switches, to the three men. "There's something draining off our power."

Not a man moved. Suddenly it didn't seem much use to move. Suddenly there wasn't much use in anything anymore.

Henessey rounded on them. "Don't stand there like mummies! Nolan, come here and examine these dials; McOrdle, take another look at the generators. You, Rumbold, for Heaven's sake stop staring and sit down."

Nobody moved.

"What's the matter with you all?" screamed Henessey.

A darkness pushed its way into the cabin. It was not that the lamps were dying, but that something was tangibly there with them. It was a force that gobbled the light from the vapor lamps before it could emerge from the tubes. It was a dark arm of space itself, invading, probing. And it was utterly, utterly alien.

The four men stood in sweat and silence. Rumbold ran his tongue over his pudgy lips. He felt the salt taste of despair and death in his mouth. There were words he wanted to speak, things about his dream and the warning that he wanted to say. He wanted to find out whether they had all dreamed the same dream; dreamed about an odd, black plane where the horizon didn't seem further away than you could reach if you stretched out your hand, and where a wraithlike form moved in the blackness towards you, and you knew that you'd come as far as you were ever going to come, ever, ever. And you knew, too, that you couldn't go back.

Henessey started shouting then.

"Get hold of yourselves can't you? I'm going to settle this once and for all. I'm starting up the superdrives in four minutes."

They moved. Slowly at first, true, but they moved. The capsules were unlocked in silence, each of them busy with his thoughts, wondering what the superdrive would do to them, but wondering still more about the other things.

Rumbold fiddled with the magno-lock on his capsule.

What was going to happen? The super drive shouldn't be used when even the normal motors were not functioning properly, surely. Yet, what would happen if they missed out on their calculations regarding precisely when the superdrives should be cut in? Henessey and McOrdle had spent seven months figuring out that point alone. To miss out by so much as a second might be fatal. But though he was thinking these things he was thinking them with only half his mind. The other half knew that it was really quite immaterial when they cut in the superdrive, quite immaterial what they did at all. Rumbold began to shiver. "We're a long way from home," he said, to no one in particular.

Nolan had the door of his capsule swinging open. He stood looking at the spotter screen. He stood looking at it for a long minute. And Nolan thought of all the things he had seen in space, the showers of meteors, the planets—Venus with its dust bowls and subterranean cities, where you could walk like a giant king among the Venusian pygmies. And he thought of all the spaceports on all the planets where he had propped up bars and drank and told stories to men whose eyes were full of wonder at the marvels of planets they had never seen.

He watched the spotter screen as if unable to look anywhere else. Space was there in that screen. And he knew space. In the cabin, everywhere else, there was something that he didn't know and didn't like. A darkness.

"Get into your capsules," said Henessey, hoarsely. "There's a minute to go."

A minute. Just one single minute of sixty single, small, infinitesimal seconds.

McOrdle stepped into his capsule and his mind was a million miles away in a small house on a hill, with a garden and chestnut trees and silver birches all around it. He saw children wandering down a narrow road on their way to school. And he saw sunsets again from his bedroom window. But it was all a million years away. It might never have been.

Three doors of three capsules closed. Henessey himself stepped into the larger capsule, which had certain control panels within it. As he stepped in he realized that he had caught a glimpse of the spotter screen. And there had been something very wrong with it. There was blackness, yes, but it was *complete* blackness. No stars, no meteors.

Nothing but darkness.

Henessey pulled a switch inside his capsule.

It reached up out of space at them and caught them as an octopus might catch a crab.

Oh, there was no sense or feeling of being caught. There was no violent deceleration. The bodies of the men in the four capsules were not torn apart. Only their minds were torn.

It was the same with each of them. A wrenching, nothing more. A single, sudden wrenching and it was all over. They felt no different, except that they knew something had happened to them. They did not know quite what. How could they?

Four doors of four capsules swung open. They stepped out.

Nolan pointed silently and they looked at where he was pointing.

The main airlock door was open and the outer door, too.

"We're grounded." whispered McOrdle.

On the control panel the instruments erratically recorded progress through space at several thousand miles per hour. Needles quivered as they had quivered before, meters recorded as they had recorded before.

And everyone knew the ship had landed, or *been* landed.

"We should be dead," said Rumbold. "We shouldn't be breathing with the ports open. We should be dead."

The four men walked over, then, to the airlock and peered out at a strange, black land that shouldn't have been there at all.

CHAPTER FOUR
Strange Dimension

"LOOK at the instruments."

"What instruments?"

"*All* the instruments."

They looked.

"It isn't possible. It just can't be."

"It's happening, isn't it?"

It was happening. They were standing in a spaceship that they could see was grounded on some strange, black asteroid; yet every instrument, every dial, every quivering needle told them that they were still travelling.

"Well, with all our instruments acting up like this it was just as well this lump of rock was here," said Rumbold.

Nolan looked at him with eyes that had seen the marvels of space a million times over. "Don't be a fool. We haven't *landed.* We couldn't have done. The deceleration would have torn us to bits."

"What do you mean, we haven't landed?" Where are we now, then, if we're not on some asteroid or other?"

"I don't know," said Nolan, simply. And the others looked at him with little fears in the shadows of their eyes.

Henessey pointed with a stubby finger. "That's land of some kind, Nolan, whatever you say. Perhaps we decelerated slowly and have not been aware of the time it has taken. Maybe we all blacked out in the capsules; maybe there was something wrong with the superdrives that cut down our speed instead of swinging us faster than light."

Nolan turned a lean face towards the mathematician. "Maybe a whole lot of things. I still don't believe we could have decelerated from the speed we were going, turned tail, and landed on our jets on an asteroid we didn't even know was here."

Henessey shrugged.

"We may as well get out and have a look at the place," said McOrdle.

"It would be a much better idea to have a look at our motors and jets. However pleasant this damned black world may turn out to be, I don't want to spend the rest of my days here," replied Henessey.

The men looked at the black world in silence. They ran their tongues over their lips and shifted their feet about. Rumbold lit a cigarette.

"Well we must do *something*," McOrdle said, tiredly.

So they took a long look at the dials telling them the speed they were travelling, the fuel they were burning, their distance from Earth and so on, and then they started to descend the long ladder down to the black ground below them.

Once on the ground each seemed afraid to go too far away from the others. It was as though they were safe only when they were together.

The black plane stretched away into the distance, yet it was foreshortened in some way and seemed scarcely a few yards in length. And the blackness of it was strangely luminous, for while there was no sun and no light save that of the stars, they were able to see each other quite well.

"Odd that the spotter didn't tell us we were nearing an asteroid," said McOrdle.

"Spotters wouldn't record a thing like this," said Rumbold, half to himself.

They knew what he meant, but none of them said anything. Each continued to stare at the plane and at the strange constellations that studded the sky above them. Then Nolan said, "I wonder what sort of stuff this is we're treading on? It looks like rock and yet, somehow…"

Henessey turned his pocket torch on it. The beam seemed to enter the surface of the plane. When he lifted the torch there was the smallest of reddish glows round the element. Just the smallest.

"Battery run out?" asked Rumbold.

"Can't have done. I only fitted new ones when we left Earth. Haven't used the thing more than a couple of times since then."

"Well, there's not much juice left in it now."

"No."

"Almost as if the rock absorbed it."

"Ridiculous," said Henessey.

"This whole place is ridiculous," said Rumbold.

"Well, will you look at *that!*" said McOrdle.

They looked.

McOrdle had bent over to pick up a pebble scarcely bigger than his fist, but the pebble would not move.

"It isn't fixed to the ground in any way that I can see, yet it won't budge an inch. What's holding it down?"

They watched him tugging at the stone. Exhausted, eventually, he stood up. The others tried to pick up stones. None of them were able to. Every pebble, no matter how small, was an integral part of the blackplane on which they were treading. And each pebble remained where it was.

"What does it mean? Why can't we move any of these stones?"

Rumbold shrugged at McOrdle's query. "Perhaps because we're not here at all; or perhaps because this place doesn't really exist."

Henessey looked at him quickly. "What are you driveling about now?"

Rumbold watched the smoke from his cigarette curling up and thought again of his dream. This was the place all right. This was the strange plane of blackness that he had seen in sleep—that, perhaps, they had all seen and were not willing to admit. "Tell me, Nolan," he said. "Did your dream have anything like this in it?" he gestured.

"In a way, yes it did. It had a plane like this in it, but I was alone. At the beginning I was alone, anyway."

"And after that—when the dream went on? What then?"

"There was a sort of wispy figure, I think. Something like…"

"Like a ghost?" rasped Henessey.

"Yes, yes, like a ghost."

"Well, there isn't any ghost here, is there? Look about you. Is there a ghost here? Can you see one? Look over there—is there one there—or there—or there? He pointed wildly in all directions. "No. There is not. Now listen to me. Wherever we are and whatever we have dreamed we are still a body of scientists with a mission. We are not schoolchildren and we are not fools. Remember that. I've had strange dreams, too, remember, but I have no intention of imagining that we are anywhere but on an asteroid that we shall shortly leave, having put our ship in order."

"It isn't the ship that's out of order," said Rumbold not to be quietened. "It's this place. It's alien—something we never banked on finding."

They were standing about on the plane, awkwardly, not knowing what to do, what to say. Suddenly they had all realized that no amount of common sense or logic or science could explain what had happened to them. Suddenly, as they felt it before in the ship, nothing mattered any more.

"Well, let's take a look around," said Nolan, just for something to say.

They started walking over the plane.

Blackness was about them, above them and below. It was a *solid* blackness, and it made a shell about each man's thoughts, making him unwilling to speak to the others of the terrors, big and small, that were crowding in upon him. For there was something about the blackness that had a note of cosmic terror more alien than anything they had ever experienced before.

Nolan was the first to break the silence.

"Did any of you notice that the stars aren't twinkling?" he said.

They looked up, all of them. Four men watching stars that were fixed, static points of light without a twinkle in them.

"Never mind that," snapped Henessey.

"*I* mind it," said Rumbold. "I'd noticed it before and didn't say anything."

"So had I," said McOrdle.

"We shouldn't be breathing," said Rumbold, and his voice was between a croak and a whisper and the others knew that he was having a hard time speaking at all without screaming. "If the stars aren't twinkling, there can't be any atmosphere on this accursed lump of rock. And humans can't live without atmosphere. And if the place is too small to have an atmosphere it must have a low gravity, yet it feels no different to Earth. Why? Why?"

Nobody knew, so nobody said anything. Henessey had given up trying to keep the others in order, because, despite his affectation of blustering rationalism, he was just as frightened as the others. Here was a lump of rock that had no business to be there, and here were four men walking, breathing, and talking without space suits to protect them from the terrible cold that by rights should have existed, without oxygen helmets and without radio communications with each other.

He gave up trying to understand.

And he was the last one to give up. The others had already done so when they first stepped out of the ship, knowing what every logical thought told them—that they couldn't live on an asteroid millions of miles from the nearest sun. But here they were—living, though some of them doubted even that.

"I wonder if we're dead," thought Nolan, feeling his arm, pinching hard just to make sure. It hurt. "If I am dead, then dead people must be able to feel, and all this doesn't feel like a dream, though…"

A dream. Could be, at that. It might have started when they went into the capsules—or even before. It could all be a continuation of the original dream. But if that were the case, then surely he would know that it was all a dream? And he did not know anything of the sort. He was *telling* himself it was a dream to keep sane. It was the only thing left to do.

Rumbold looked back over his shoulder at the ship. It seemed almost to have merged with the blackness of the plane. It took him a few seconds to focus his eyes properly in order to see it at all. Almost as though it's going to fade away altogether, he thought. Almost as though the last link is breaking, the last, very last thing which holds us to the past, holds us to Earth. Soon there won't be any links left. Soon we shall just be here on this black plane, without anything behind us at all; no past, no ship, no Earth. How soon would it happen, he wondered? Perhaps in a second's time. Perhaps this was the last second in which he could live and breathe and remember. But no. See—he could still remember. It hasn't happened yet, he mused. But it is bound to happen soon. And after that—what then? What is going to happen to us when our past is forgotten? Is there some sort of future planned for us? Is this the afterlife? Are we dead men refusing to realize that we are dead? Is that what it all means? Questions, questions—all the time these questions running about in his head like spiders in a dark coal shed.

The four men walked slowly. They threw no shadows as they walked, for there was no sun, no moon, no source of light at all, yet somehow they could see where they were going and could make out the plane quite clearly. They walked in silence now. Not a word was spoken. Not a word. Silently, as dead men, they walked, perhaps believing themselves dead, yet not being quite sure. Sometimes one of them would look back at the ship, just making sure that it was still there. Just making certain that all the links had not been broken.

Then one of the men spoke. It was Henessey.

"Look boys. I know we all feel the same. I know we're all puzzled, maybe think we're dead and so on. But this walking isn't helping us at all. It's not getting us anywhere. We're not finding out anything about this place and we're not likely to. We're getting further and further away from the ship all the time and—well, I for one want to leave this place *some* time."

It was a good try. Rumbold and McOrdle looked at the little mathematician and wondered whether he still believed in what he was saying or whether he was talking just to keep his own spirits up.

Nolan was walking a little behind the others. His voice came softly in answer to Henessey. "Did I hear you say something about the ship, Henessey?"

"You did. I said that we were getting further and further away when we should be back there seeing what repairs are needed."

Nolan gave a sharp little laugh, but when they looked at him they saw that his eyes were not laughing. "Take a look back there," he said.

They looked back, all of them. There was a black plane almost, but not quite, merging with a black sky.

There wasn't any spaceship.

They stood staring, badly shaken towards the empty space where their ship had been. No one spoke for several minutes. Then:

"Well, that's that," said Henessey. "What do you suppose happened and where are we?"

Rumbold shrugged. "Does it matter? We're not leaving. There's no hurry."

McOrdle scratched his ear, pursed his mouth. "Ever think that the effect of the superdrive might have done something? Mathematically it merely increased our speed to faster-than-light. But supposed it had some effect on our speed in *another* direction."

Eager to talk, Nolan turned on the little engineer. "What are you getting at?"

"Remember Stillwater's papers on the fourth dimensional aspects of speed and time ratios? He spent his whole life trying to prove that mass increased in relation to all speeds faster than light, but increased *outside* the three known dimensions into the fourth. Perhaps something like that happened to us."

"That doesn't explain what happened to our ship before the superdrive was cut in," said Rumbold.

"You mean the lights and the dials jumping and all that?"

"Yes. And it doesn't explain the dreams, either."

"Well," said Nolan. "You're the psychologist. Aren't psychologists supposed to be well up in dreams?"

Rumbold glowered. "When I started talking about dreams before, I was called a lunatic. I don't want it to happen again."

"Never mind that. You tell me what you think about your dream. Was it anything like all this?"

"Yes, it was—it was the same dream as yours. The black plane, the wispy figure. Everything."

"Anything else besides?"

Rumbold strained his mind, remembering. "Yes—I think there was some sort of building behind the figure. But I couldn't be sure."

"It was the same in my dream. Some sort of building." Rumbold nodded. "I thought it would be. We all dreamed the same thing, didn't we?" He looked at Henessey, at McOrdle.

They nodded in unison.

"So where does that get us?" countered Henessey.

"It means that whatever happened to us started before the superdrives were cut in. So McOrdle's theory about speed and the fourth dimension doesn't hold water. No. All this has nothing to do with physics, I'm sure of that."

"Off on your ghosts again, Rumbold?" Henessey said it with a sneer.

"Not ghosts necessarily, no. What I mean is this—we all had dreams and they were all the same dream, right?"

"Right."

"You might call them collective hallucinatory dreams if you want to. But more important than that they were *prophetic* dreams. What we dreamed is coming to pass. Here we are on the black plane. Right here and now it's happening to us. Now you could still say that the dreams were simply premonitions of what was to come—then you can accept McOrdle's theory of the fourth dimension. But I think you'd be wrong to do so."

Nolan had been looking away into the dark distance. He turned and said, "What's your view, then, Rumbold?"

"I think that we should have found ourselves here whether we had used the superdrive or not. Probably we *are* in the fourth dimension, or at any rate in some other plane of existence. But my point is this—we were scheduled to come here at a specific moment regardless of super drive effects or anything else."

"Scheduled?" That was Henessey.

"Yes, scheduled. Something planned all this with a definite purpose."

"And that purpose?" queried Henessey.

"I don't know," said Rumbold.

"Look," said Nolan.

And there, in the distant dark, almost merging with the sky, yet visible apart from it, was a building.

"A laboratory," said Nolan.

"A cathedral," said Rumbold.

"A palace," said McOrdle.

"Where, where—what are you talking about?" said Henessey, wildly staring, leaning forward as though by so doing he could make out the building.

"The building, the building over there." Rumbold held Henessey's arm and pointed.

But Henessey never saw a thing.

The others did, though.

For Nolan it was a mighty laboratory; a huge building of black concrete and glittering crystal. He felt it *had* to be a laboratory. It reared up into the sky and he wondered why he had not noticed it before, it being so tall and mighty. It had vast stretches of windows and observation towers and ramps where scouting ships might once have sat. Oh, it was a mighty place indeed! He wondered what manner of people built this building and he found their images forming in his mind. A frightening race of creatures unlike any other. Quite unlike.

And that was how Nolan saw it.

For Rumbold things were different. The building was a glorious cathedral sending spires up into the dark. It was a dream cathedral of power and majesty, with stained glass windows and the sound of organ music bursting from its giant walls. It was almost like one of the great old buildings of the early days, dead and buried now beneath the rubble of two atomic wars.

The building was a palace for McOrdle. A palace from the fairy tale books with pointed towers and flights of vast steps leading up, up, up...

The three of them were almost convinced, now, that they were dead.

And for Henessey there was no building at all.

"You're mad, mad, *mad!*" he screamed. "All of you are mad. There isn't anything there. There's a black plane and that's all. Nothing else at all. Nothing."

"Nothing for you, perhaps," said Rumbold.

"What do you mean?"

"What I say. If we are in the fourth dimension and if this whole thing was planned with a purpose, then we are each seeing what we expect to see. To each of us the building is different. I see a cathedral; Nolan sees a laboratory, and so on. Because you are still clinging to logic you see nothing."

"Then I'm the only sane one here. You're all having hallucinations. That's what's happening. You're breaking up. All of you." He only stopped when he found he was screaming.

The four men carried on walking across the plane towards the laboratory, the cathedral, the palace and towards nothing at all.

CHAPTER FIVE
Suspicion

PERHAPS thirty seconds had passed since Waring had gone back. Yyrmac stood beside the Time Brain, with the other Martians at his elbow. He stood silently, stroking his face with twig-like fingers.

It had all been done in such a rush that he had hardly had time to think it over before. But now... How strange it had all been. Strange enough to make him suspicious.

First of all the arrival of NNgar at his office. NNgar, one of the heads of the Government, arriving in a private hovercar to pay a personal call. That in itself had been unusual.

"You are friendly with the Earthman Charles Talbot Wade?"

"That's right."

"He may contact you with a proposition regarding use of the Time Brain. Probably in the very near future. Today even. As you know, Wade is a great friend of ours and a prominent man on Earth. In the interests of Free Trade— and for other reasons—we should do all we can to help him. Even if it means going against our normal practices regarding the use of the Time Brain."

"But surely—the Science Council will not agree."

"I'm afraid I cannot give you any information of the official attitude of the Council. However, as Wade will probably contact you, since you are known to him personally. I have been instructed to give you complete freedom of movement to help him."

"And am I supposed to tell him that you have spoken to me?"

"Definitely not. Wade will be under the impression that he has had an idea and will need your help in carrying it out—in actual fact he will have been *given* an idea. He must still think that it is his own and you will have to give him the impression that your help is unofficial. Under no circumstances must he or anyone else connected with the business find out that the Government know anything. Probably someone from Earth will come over to use the Brain. You will have to tell him that you are doing the Earth people a favor because you hope Wade will help in the crusade for free Trade—some story like that."

Yrmac had nodded. "Yes, I see. By the way—do you know what it is that Wade will ask me—apart from wanting to use the Time Brain. What do they want the Brain to tell them?"

NNgar had looked Yrmac straight in the eyes. "They have found a part of their interstellar ship in space. They want to find out what happened to it."

"But—"

"There are no 'buts.' The orders of our Government are that we should help them to find out anything they wish to know—but only by letting them use the Time Brain. They must not know that we are aware of what happened to their ship. They must find out everything for themselves."

And there the interview had ended. Yrmac had heard from Wade that night. It had all been just as NNgar had said; the Newscreen man wanted to send one of his reporters with the fragment of the first interstellar ship. He had agreed to help and had met Waring, the reporter, as planned. From then on it had been easy. Very easy. And now he had time to think about it all. What *did* it mean? Why had NNgar said that he had been "instructed?" Did that mean that the orders had come from Supreme Office or the President? And why were the Government letting the Earthmen use the Time Brain for such a purpose—did they have some plan in wanting the Earthmen to find out about the stars and what lay up there?

Yyrmac watched the glowing Brain, imagining himself in Waring's place, and in the place of those other Earthmen who had set off for the first voyage to the stars. And Yyrmac shuddered a long shudder, his brittle blue body shimmering with uneasiness.

Charles Talbot Wade stood at the great crystal window of his office and looked out at the red rocket trails burning pencil streamers in the sky.

Looking back on it all he could see how strange, how phony it had all been. First the incredible luck attached to the finding of the fragment of the *Sunderling* by Van Carlsberg. That had started him off, and in haste he had fixed up with Yyrmac to send Waring over to Mars to use the Time Brain. That had all been too easy. Much too easy. Then Waring had gone and his first inkling of doubt arrived. He had become suspicious of the thing and had had Van Carlsberg investigated. The little spaceman had never been near Titan during the past six months, yet that was where he had said he had picked up the fragment. Van Carlsberg had, in fact, come straight from Mars on a Martian ship, which had left immediately. Presumably he had brought the bit of the *Sunderling* from Mars with him, which meant that the Martians knew about the *Sunderling*. Perhaps *they* had found the lump of metal in space. And why all this secrecy anyway? What were the Marties up to? He trusted Yyrmac as a friend, yet he knew the strict hold the Martian Government and Science Council had on its members.

The Newscreen building shuddered as the night ship left the field for Venus. Watching, Wade saw the night grow bright and dark again as the ship blasted off. He stirred his coffee absently, drank it down in a gulp. A thousand thousand worries buzzed in his head like blowflies, settling, then up again and buzzing all the more. What was Van Carlsberg's place in all this? Did he stand to gain in some obscure way? Were the Martians hiring his services? That seemed the most likely bet. Obviously the thing to do was to get hold of Van Carlsberg and find out what part he had played in this—he sought for a word—this conspiracy. Now was it a conspiracy, his cautious self questioned? Well, if not a conspiracy it was quite obviously some sort of plan. But who was the plan directed against? Earth? Newscreen?

He punctured a hole in the end of a cigar and lit it, turning the match this way and that. The fact is, he thought, you can't trust anybody. Not even a veteran spaceman like Van Carlsberg—though if he had been lying why had the desk psycho recorder not reacted?

But all this was getting him nowhere. Either he must wait until Waring returned from Mars or he must do some personal investigations right away.

He paced the floor of his office, blowing smoke out into the room. The stillness of the building seemed suddenly oppressive. He had the feeling that something was going on that he ought to know about. Something big.

He thought about Waring—by now all connected up to the Time Brain and travelling with Henessey and his men towards the stars. And for some reason the thought of that depressed him still further.

He stopped pacing. Either he needed a drink or else…

He walked to the visor.

The robot brunette gleamed a plastic smile at him.

"The Spaceport," he snapped.

"Interplanetary at your service," said a tired voice.

"Charles Wade here. Get my ship ready within half an hour."

The voice made itself less tired. The face tried to look alert and intelligent. Where to, Mr. Wade?"

"Mars," said Wade and clicked the switch. The screen blanked out.

CHAPTER SIX
The Guardian

THEY walked towards the building silently. It wasn't that they *couldn't* talk, but just that there seemed no need to do so.

The building lay waiting for them to come. The building that was a cathedral, a palace, a laboratory and the building that never existed, waited for them in black silence. Perhaps it had sat there for a million million centuries, thought Rumbold. Or perhaps it had been built in a minute, an hour, a day. Perhaps it was only there at all because they expected to see it.

The building lay waiting.

"It looks so *old,*" said McOrdle.

Nolan looked hurt, somehow. "Nonsense. It's new."

"It's both—or neither," said Rumbold.

And Henessey said nothing at all.

The cathedral was on a high mound, Rumbold noticed. There was a flight of broad stone steps leading up to it and from the building itself he could hear some sort of music. Organ music, it sounded like. He started to climb the steps, the others slightly behind him. On either side of the great wooden door stone towers rose to scrape their fingers on the black ceiling of space. Oh, it was a giant place, a cathedral such as Rumbold had never seen before; and it looked so incredibly *old,* as old, Rumbold thought, as time itself. But then, of course, that meant nothing here, where time was forgotten, tucked away somewhere for the long night. No, there was no time at all here on the asteroid; no time and no reason for time to exist. And the cathedral was timeless also.

Above the door the giant Cyclops eye of a stained-glass window winked down at them. Rumbold smiled, wondering quietly what the others saw where he saw a stained-glass window. And he wondered, too, whether Henessey would eventually see anything.

Nolan was walking slightly behind the psychologist and wondering why he was taking such odd steps—almost as though he was walking up stairs of some kind. He shrugged. There were too many things about this that he didn't understand. So many things, in fact, that he had given up trying. The laboratory was one of them. Who had built it and for what reason? And how could a laboratory be built at all in what they had all come to believe must be the fourth dimension? And such a huge place it was, too. Vast columns of black stone and glittering crystal windows everywhere, and not a sign of anyone living or working in it. Supposing there was someone inside, though; what would they *look* like? Would they have thirty heads and a thousand metal hands? Would they be like the grey-green fungous creatures of the Venusian caverns, or like the pigmy Venusians themselves? Or perhaps they would be frail and blue like the Martians. Or they might even be human.

McOrdle sniffed. He fancied that he caught the scent of spices or incense drifting from the castle as he walked up the winding causeway behind Rumbold and Nolan. Yes, there it was again! A fragrance, an odor! It told of palaces and kings and mystery, of strange hidden lands beyond the farthest seas, the farthest spaces. It was the smell of ancient and eternal things that brooded away the centuries in dim, dark corners of the universe. So this was it at last, then. Heaven, hell, the fourth dimension—what did it matter? This was IT–that was all that mattered. The end of the line, the finish; the cutting of the last slim thread, the dying of the flame. He felt he wanted to laugh, but he knew what the others would think of him if he did. But to hell with the others. It didn't matter now, did it?

"Ha ha!" he laughed.

Nolan turned. "What's up with you?"

"Just laughing."

"I know you were laughing. What at?"

"Things."

"What things? I can't see anything to laugh at here."

"I wasn't laughing at anything *here*. Oh, no. I was laughing at things back on Earth. How far away is that, by the way?"

"What are you getting at?"

Nolan smiled a sly smile. "You see—you can't tell me, can you? You don't know how far away Earth is. None of us knows. It might be a million miles, it might be right *here.*" He reached out and grasped a handful of air. "If we're in another dimension we might be on Earth at this very minute. We might be walking down Shaftesbury Avenue, London, or down Fifth Avenue, or along the top of the Great Wall of China. All places may co-exist with another place in another dimension. And will you tell me this—what does time mean in the fourth dimension? Anything or nothing? And supposing it has no meaning—what then? On Earth at this moment a dinosaur might be feeding where in another so many million years of Earth time someone will be, or is, or was drinking coffee at a kiosk in Trafalgar Square."

Henessey pulled a pocket torch from his suit. "Look, McOrdle. This is a torch—you've seen it before. I press a button—so. And light emerges. Right?"

"Well?"

"Supposing that had been a pistol pointing at my head. Would I have died? *Can* one die in the fourth dimension?"

"Perhaps we're dead already."

Henessey ignored the remark. "Look—if there are *four* dimensions and if we *have* been transferred into the fourth in some way, then what about death? Can we be killed, or can't we?"

"Gentlemen…" said a voice.

"Who said that," screamed Henessey, turning.

The others were all looking at something that had come between them and the black building. A wispy figure—almost, indeed, a wraith.

"Rumbold, Nolan, McOrdle—what are you *looking* at?"

"Just the same as the dream," breathed Nolan.

"Yes, yes. Just the same," said the other two, softly, to themselves.

The shadowy figure stood, wavering, on the steps of the cathedral, on the causeway of the palace, on the quadrangle before the laboratory. It wisped, fluctuated, and shivered like a figure of smoke. It seemed for a moment to be faintly luminous, then as dark as the plane, as dark as space.

Slowly it took form.

Nolan found himself looking at a cross between a human, a Venusian and a Martian.

For Rumbold it was a priest that took form.

And McOrdle saw a tall man dressed in robes of gold.

Henessey looked at nothing and started to shiver.

"Please follow me," said the priest, the king, the alien and empty space. The four men walked into the building.

And, as with the outside, so with the inside of the place; it was different for each of them.

As he walked behind the others, Henessey started to *believe*. Up until that moment he had been telling himself constantly that everything, though strange, could be explained rationally. The voice was more than he could stomach, however. It made him shake inside himself; a sort of inward quaking as though acids were lustily at work on his bones and his organs, eating everything away swiftly, swiftly. Slowly the voice began to have a body, summoned up from the chasms of his own subconscious, as were the visions of the others, Rumbold, Nolan, and McOrdle. Yes, a body was forming.

He watched closely, feeling his mouth dropping open and not bothering to close it. The figure was that of a tall, strong man, in a white coat. And as the figure's outlines became filled in with substance, as the body grew out of wispiness and smoke, so the air hummed and gathered itself in, solidified, slanted, soared, angled and twisted into walls and doorways.

Henessey stood in a long narrow room, with the three other men and the stranger in the white coat. The room had many doors leading off it, and each of the doors had a small aperture, fitted with bars.

Bars... A man in a white coat... Bars....

A madhouse.

Henessey screamed a shrill high scream and turned. His feet clattered on the metal floor. At the end of the room a corridor led away into another part of the building. Henessey plunged down it, hearing the voices of his friends calling him back ringing like a death knell in his ears. No—he would not go back. He must get out of the building—out anywhere away from this terror.

The corridor branched and he paused for a moment, undecided. No sound of pursuit came to his ears and the voices of Rumbold and the others had faded. Nothing stirred anywhere. There was no sound at all, only the irregular whistling of his own breathing.

Which way to go now? He gazed down each of the corridors in turn, poised, ready to be off at any small sound.

The left hand corridor seemed to have a rubber floor and be judged that that one probably led into the building. The metal-floored passage was more likely to lead to a door. He padded swiftly down the right hand corridor, pausing every now and then to listen. But there was no sound of pursuit.

Fear fluttered in his stomach like a bat awakening in a dark cave. It crept through him, exploring his arms and causing them to tremble, exploring his legs and causing them to shake even as he walked. And the fear came into his mind, too. When he felt it there he knew that it had come never to go away again.

Then whatever it was that had kept him so silent, so careful, dropped away from him as cigarette smoke curls in a room and suddenly is gone.

His screams hurled themselves back at him from the walls of the endless corridors down which he ran. They came back at him in fury and in mad bursts of sound, echoes, and reverberations thundering in his skull until it seemed the bones of his head must balloon out and snap into a thousand white and calcinated fragments.

'Down *this* corridor he ran and then down *that* corridor, through this arch and through that door, across this room and into the next, always with the sound of his screaming billowing in hideous gusts in his wake.

Sometimes, too, it seemed that his own screams were waiting for him when he opened the door of a fresh room. The walls would make themselves into mouths and shout in madness and fear. And when he turned to run the other way it was as though the mouths constricted and made obscene tittering sounds behind their hands that were the closing doors.

Twenty-thirty-half a hundred rooms and corridors heard his voice and his clattering feet.

Then he saw a small window in the wall of one of the corridors. He slowed up, panting, falling against the wall. The window was about five or six feet up. He could reach it easily.

He bent his legs, then straightened them, springing like some panic-stricken bullfrog. His fingers fastened on the small sill of the window and he scraped his feet against the wall, hoisting himself up. The window was of dark blue plastic, with an automatic catch. He pressed the button and the window swung open.

Beyond the window lay another corridor, just like all the others.

Tears came blindingly into his eyes, the saltiness of them coming eventually to his mouth as they ran down his cheeks, rivulets of despair.

Squeezing through the narrow window he dropped to the rubbery floor and made off once more, by this time having no idea of which way to go or the way he had come. But somewhere, *surely,* there must be a door, an exit.

Purposely he stopped himself from thinking about what he would do when and if he found a door. Would the space ship still be there? And if it was there, would he try to get away on his own or would he attempt to rescue his friends? Thoughts like these he trod viciously underfoot with every step he took.

Was that a sound? He stopped, one foot raised like a stork. His body shook with a secret, inner trembling. A trembling and a shaking such as he had never known before came over him and through him like a wind among trees, fleetingly. Then it was gone.

Silence.

He had stopped screaming now, but without knowing it. He stood a moment to regain his breath. *Flee, flee,* whispered a million voices from the walls, from the rubbery floor, from the doors, from the drear silences of the building.

At the end of the corridor there was another door. Perhaps that one led outside. It seemed to be bigger than the others through which he had come. There was just a chance...

He padded softly, oh, so softly, down towards the door. It was a grey door, smooth and blandly smiling, or so it seemed. He gripped the handle, paused, then pushed. The door opened.

"I could have told you it was useless to run," said the man in the white coat.

And Rumbold, McOrdle, and Nolan stared at him, pityingly.

Henessey crumpled and fell, like the falling of a tower of child's bricks. But he had not fainted. He lay on the floor of the room with his eyes open and his mouth twitching silently. His head was crookedly turned towards the others and he watched them with an unblinking stare.

Suddenly an idea occurred to him. "How long have I been gone?" he asked, croakingly.

"Why," said Nolan. "You went out of one door and came in the other. Just like that. You haven't been away any time."

"Hardly more than a second," said Rumbold.

"No time at all," said McOrdle.

For them I have hardly been away, thought Henessey, there on the floor. But for me, for me...

The man in the white coat looked at him with pity. "Time is only an illusion, after all," he said.

"Then we are in another dimension?" This from Nolan.

"Another plane, yes."

"But why? What reason have you for keeping us here? How did we come to this place, anyway? And the dreams we all had…"

The alien creature waved its tentacles vaguely at Nolan. "It is a long and complicated story," it said. "You are here because you cannot go any further. If you like to say that you are in the fourth dimension—well, you could do worse than think along those lines. As for the dreams—to explain those you would have to understand the nature of the particular plane of existence in which you now find yourself. You know, I presume, that the sub-conscious is more receptive to, shall we say, things psychic, than is the conscious? Naturally, therefore, when you slept the conscious slipped away and the supersensitive sub-conscious took over. At the moment of your sleeping I was *arranging* for your capture. In your dreams you were receptive to my intentions and automatically saw what you saw. You were not sufficiently put out by the visions to turn your ship and return to Earth. No, you came on. Therefore you had to be taken."

Rumbold looked at the priest strangely. Before this venerable figure he felt a little awed. He wanted to speak, to ask a thousand questions, but the words tangled up with themselves before he could utter them. Eventually he said, "But what reason have you for wanting us here?"

"You must be prevented from going on."

"Why, though. Why?"

"That I shall tell you in good time."

"This place, then," Rumbold waved his arms. "Has it always been here? Is it old, new, ageless?"

The priest's eyes grew kindly. "It will be difficult for you to understand when I tell you that this place is not here in the material sense. Not here at all."

"But I can see it. I can feel it. Look." And Rumbold bent down and touched the floor of the cathedral nave, banging the ancient stone with his hand. "And I can smell the smell of incense burning, too," He sniffed and the waves of incense burned in his nostrils, sweetly.

The priest pointed to Henessey. "He now believes this place is real, but he did not at one time. This building took form about his head as soon as he started to believe in its existence. Does that not prove what I am trying to tell you?"

"Then you created this building?"

"I merely put the idea of the building into your minds. It was your own thoughts that made it what you see. This place is really no more than a shadow, given substance by your own minds. You see it as a cathedral. The others see it differently."

"Then," said Rumbold, "if I close my eyes and refuse to believe in its existence it will go like so much smoke and dreams. I can will it away."

The priest shook his head. "You already believe in it. You cannot wholeheartedly disbelieve something that has once had shape and form for you."

McOrdle looked at the man in regal robes before him. "What I don't understand," he said, "is why we are here. If you say you brought us here because we could not be allowed to go further towards the stars, then that implies that you have the power to do whatever you want with us. Why then all this fourth dimension stuff? Why did you not simply destroy us or send our ship off at a tangent, alter our course so that we missed our destination by a few millions of miles?"

The gold robes rustled. "I did not alter your course for one reason only. If you had gone on travelling through space with your superdrive you would eventually have reached some other system. Your bodies by that time might well have become rust, but the ship would have gone on and there was the chance that it would have been discovered."

"Discovered?" Despite his feeling that all was over, finished, McOrdle could not help a jump of his, heart, a tingling of his blood. "Then there is life up there?"

The man in the gold robes smiled. "Yes, there is life," he said. "Life in a million different forms unknown to you people of Earth."

"But if there is life, what is wrong with us going to find it?" said Rumbold. "Surely since we have the superdrive we could have reached the stars and their planets—we could have discovered this life you speak about."

"Exactly. You not only could have, but you would have discovered it."

Nolan addressed the alien being. "From your tone I take it that we are not going to be allowed to continue with our plans?"

"I'm afraid that is the case."

"And who or what are you? What right have you to stop us from doing what we planned to do? Why have you done what you have done?"

"Yes, why?" queried the others.

And so there in that dark building that was a cathedral, a laboratory, a palace, and a madhouse, the being that had the shape of a priest, an alien creature, a king, and an asylum attendant, told them of the secrets of the stars...

CHAPTER SEVEN
Secret of the Stars

THE being looked at each of them in turn, and his eyes told them that what they were going to hear would not be pleasant. Its voice came to each of them, as from a great distance.

"You ask me why you cannot go further towards the stars. The answer to that is not a pleasant thing. In fact, for a race that has progressed as far as you have it is decidedly unpleasant. But you are here to learn and therefore I must tell you...

"With your superdrive ship you can cover the distances of space and reach other galaxies, other worlds. But though you are capable of doing this, capable of overcoming all the technical problems of interstellar flight, you are *not* capable of keeping your own world in order. For instance—some ten years ago there was a threat of a war between Mats and Earth. There is still considerable friction within the Earth Government to this day, some still feel that war with Mars is necessary and, in fact, desirable. What does that suggest to you?"

Rumbold blew his nose. The others looked at the floor. No one essayed an answer, for there didn't seem any answer to give. The being was quite right in what he was saying. Too right.

"You do not answer me because you know that what I am saying is not pleasant, yet it is true. You on Earth have progressed since the nineteenth century with remarkable speed, but you have progressed in one direction only. You are like the freak who grows to about nine or ten feet and then finds that his legs can hardly support the weight of his body. Your technical capabilities show intensive progress along that single, and narrow, line. But the truth of the matter IS that you are not yet grown up. You are still in your adolescence. And nobody trusts an adolescent with an atom bomb."

McOrdle looked puzzled. "All that you say may be true, but…"

"It is true."

"Perhaps. But it does not show us *why* we are being prevented from reaching the stars. We are not going there with a shipload of atomic bombs or war dust. When we went to Venus and Mars it was as explorers and scientists, not as warmongers."

The gold robes rustled as the being leaned towards Me-Ordle, smiling. "And what happened on Venus? You set up atomic piles, cosmic radiation testing plants, radioactive war dust conserves. The atomic piles blew up—or one of them did, and you decimated the Venusian pygmies because you didn't know that the screens that protected you from the cosmic radiations were insufficient to protect them."

"Yes—but take Mars…"

"Mars refuses to allow large numbers of your people on her planet. The Martians are wise people."

Henessey had been on his feet for some time, staring glassily at the white-coated figure. "So you're telling us we're animals?" he said, scarcely above a whisper, his mouth working.

"Not at all. I'm saying that humans are adolescent. As a race they have a long, long way to go."

"Before what?"

"Before they will be fit to go to the stars and the other worlds of the stars."

Henessey's eyes were wide, two diamonds glinting in a light that came from nowhere and illuminated a place that never should have been. "And you say there is life up there?"

"Have you ever examined a drop of pond water under a microscope? Have you ever watched all the myriad creatures that swim and turn, pulsate and dive, dash and crawl? Oh, yes, there is life up there. Lots of life, some of it intelligent, some of it not, some of it good and some of it evil, some of it, even, adolescent."

"And we can't go on? Can't see it?"

"That's right. You can't see it."

Henessey buried his face in his hands. A snuffling came from him, a dull, childish sound. To think of it—so near they had come, so near. And there was life up there. Not just barren planets and sparkling suns revolving endlessly in space. Not just these things, but life. And he would never see it. All his dreams...

"And who are you to stop us?" McOrdle asked the question that had been in all their minds.

"Merely a Guardian."

"A Guardian of what?"

"Of the stars, of the people who live on the other planets, even of humanity."

"Are you real?"

"As real as you have made me."

Nolan peered intently at the alien. "Are there more of your kind in this place or are you the only one?"

"I am the only one here. It was not thought that more than one would be necessary."

Rumbold stabbed a finger. "You said 'It was not thought.' By that you must mean that there *are* others?"

The priest nodded slowly. "There are others. Not like me, however. I am simply the personification of a force."

"In other words, you are simply a weapon being used by some other race against us?"

"You could say that."

"And what is this other race, then? Are they from the stars?"

The priest shook his head. "Not as you understand the stars, no. They are the Planners, the Guardians, the Masters."

"What do you mean? What are you getting at?"

"Have you never thought that life might not be the indiscriminate jumble that it appears? Have you never wondered whether there was some sort of planning done, some reason behind life? Earlier in the days of Earth humanity *believed*. They were nearer the truth then. Now your religion has become a series of traditions, customs, and ceremonies. The belief is no longer there. But at one time the Planners thought you were going to progress along the right lines."

"What are these Planners?"

"A race."

"But what sort of race? Where do they live, what are they like?"

"A million centuries before your world was born they had already mapped the form Earth life was to take. That is how powerful they are. Where do they live? They live in space, if you like to put it that way. They exist now to keep their eyes on the universe, to plan, to watch, to guard, to alter, to experiment. And that is not all. Sometimes they must destroy."

"Why?"

"Because while they like to let evolution patterns take their own form there are times when it is impossible. Let me tell you of one instance. On a certain planet on the outskirts of the Crab Nebula a race evolved; not very swiftly. The Planners had planted the seed and they watched it grow. The race was unlike anything that you have seen, so I will not attempt to describe it to you. These beings progressed at normal rate until one of their scientists evolved a method of speeding up the evolutionary pattern by mutation. Within three centuries there were seven different stages of evolution on that planet, each one subject to the one above it. The highest evolved a method of teleportation that would have enabled them to bridge space at will. Then the Planners stepped in. For this race was basically evil. The Planners sent a plague. There are only a thousand odd beings left on that planet now, all in a lower evolutionary bracket."

"That is their custom, then? To interfere?"

"By no means. They interfere only when it is necessary. They are aware of the consequences of letting a race get too advanced along a certain path. Knowing the variety of patterns the future may take they are able to select the best one and adjust conditions accordingly. They do not interfere just for the pleasure of doing so, if that is what you are thinking."

A silence came, then. Each of the men was thinking of the Planners, the Masters, the Watchers. The invincible powers that governed everything. Yes, thought Rumbold, the ancients had been right in their beliefs.

The building was a silent tomb for all of them. They stood like dead men, their arms hanging limply down beside them, their eyes filled with a mixture of understanding and amazement, horror and belief. For they knew that what they were being told was true, correct. They knew and yet did not want to know, they believed and yet did not want to believe.

Rumbold laughed with his mind as he thought of the old philosophy that man was master of his own destiny. And yet, he thought, it *is* true in a way. The Planners do not interfere unless they have to. But they are interfering now. They have brought us to this place to prevent us from going on towards the stars. They think we are adolescent. Adolescent! And another part of his mind said, "Well, aren't we?"

Nolan ran a thick tongue round his mouth. "Look," he said. "If the Planners wanted to stop us getting to the stars, why didn't they simply destroy Henessey before he discovered the superdrive?"

"Because if Henessey hadn't discovered the superdrive when he did, it would have been discovered four years afterwards by Clantering."

Henessey looked up. "Clantering—?"

"Yes. He was due to discover the principle of the superdrive if you had not done so."

Nolan grunted, then said, "Couldn't this man Clantering have been destroyed as well?"

The alien creature nodded its alien head at Nolan. "Certainly he could. But you cannot kill every scientist who decides to work on speeds faster than light without somebody getting suspicious. The Planners could, of course, have removed Clantering and Henessey and any others by obliterating them from the memory of all who knew them, but that again is against the Planners' fundamental ideas. They have no *wish* to interfere at all, but sometimes interference is necessary. That is the case now."

"But I don't see why they *want* to interfere," said Rumbold to the priest.

The priest turned. "You don't? But surely it is obvious. The Planners, being aware of what is happening on the many different worlds, must keep their eyes on all developments to ensure that the best possible future is chosen and worked out. There is an infinity of possibilities so far as the future is concerned, as you know. The Planners want to ensure that the best becomes the *actual* future."

"Best for whom?"

"For everyone, of course. There are other worlds to be considered besides Earth and Venus and Mars. Your superdrive gives you interstellar flight, but if you had seen, as the

Planners saw, some of the possibilities that were laid down, resulting solely from your spaceship's successful first flight— why then you would have been appalled. And what is more, you would have destroyed the superdrive."

"Words, words," said Henessey. "Nothing but words. You tell us these things expecting us to believe them? How can any race know the patterns of the future?"

"They are aware of your disbelief, Henessey," said the man in the white coat. "And for this reason they have instructed me to show you all something of what might happen." He smiled, then corrected himself, "What might *have* happened."

He led the way into another rom. Nolan looked about him at vast banks of apparatus, screens, tubes, maps.

Rumbold saw a small chancel. There was a stained glass window on one wall.

McOrdle gazed at a crystal ball set on a silver table.

Henessey's room was small and grey and silent. There was a simple window at eye level, small also.

"Look," said the being, pointing. They looked at the screen, the stained glass window, the crystal ball, and the plain window.

A cloudiness came, a mist. It cleared and they saw a vast council chamber a mile in height. Great toad-like creatures sat on stone slabs, all of them taller than the tallest tree of Earth. A few human figures, ants among these colossi, walked up and down.

"That is the result of the Earthmen landing on Caroola, second planet of the sun Pyyth. Humans soon found that the planet was rich in radioactive elements. They also discovered that these giant toad-like creatures were intelligent and wanted no truck with Earth. Naturally the human race wasn't to be told to go. It then set to work devising a weapon by which a peaceful race could be subjected. The weapon was sound. These creatures' auditory system is far more sensitive than that of any creatures in the Solar system. Despite their bulk they are quite silent. High-pitched sounds affect their ears and nerves and what passes for a heart in a fatal way. Humans were not long in finding that out and making good use of it. In this way an intelligent race is stopped in its growth. Its evolution is cut off. It becomes a slave race. See—again—"

Once more the cloudiness. Then a view of a planet covered with fiery scars, running with liquid rock, plumed with billows of smoke, scabbed with the bodies of toad-like things.

"The eventual destruction of the race. The radioactive metals are tested. Has Earth got a weapon that can be used from a great distance and is yet capable of destroying an entire planet? It has. To prove it, it destroys a complete planet, Caroola, second planet of the sun Pyyth.

"That is one of the possibilities. There are others."

And the cloudiness came again and again, each time clearing to show a fresh aspect of man's power and might among the far reaches of the universe. Each one showed something new, some showed cruelty, some simply ignorance, some showed war, others famine and plague. All were horrible.

"You mean all those happenings are going to come about if man reaches the stars?" queried Nolan, sweat on his forehead like a row of glass beads.

"No. If your voyage was successful, if man reached the stars now, at his present level of development, then these are some of the things that are laid down in the patterns of the future as *possible* events. There are infinitely more different possibilities than I could show you if I cared to hold you here for a century of your time."

Henessey looked away from the screen. Was this creature to be believed? "But these things are only possibilities. You are not showing us what will happen, but only what might.

Yet on the grounds of what might happen you are ready to prevent us from going on."

"Naturally. As I said, these are only a few of the things that I have shown you. There are others. There are so many others that it is not worth the risk of allowing you go ahead. You and your race, Henessey, are not sufficiently adult to deal with the things you will find on these other worlds. In another five or six centuries, perhaps, but not now. Humanity is a little boy with a powerful rifle; if you cannot take the rifle away from him you must prevent him from shooting anybody with it. That is the view of the Planners."

"What about all the good things on Earth? What about all the great philosophers, artists, writers?" said Nolan.

The alien turned to him, saying, "Well, what about the good things? Most of the great artists, writers, and philosophers are already dead and nothing new, artistic or beautiful has emerged from your illustrious planet for a large number of years. No, Nolan, the technical accomplishments of the human race are great, but as for anything else—" The alien shuddered.

"Have the Planners prevented other races from journeying to other planets and other galaxies?" asked Henessey.

"Of course. It is going on all the time."

"All the time," murmured Henessey. To think that a million races were all probably imagining that they were the sole intelligent beings in the universe, yet feeling that there might be life on other worlds, and all the time the Planners were preventing them from ever finding out. He thought of the stars outside, blobs of light on a black velvet curtain, and he felt a strange sense of affinity towards the beings up there, whatever they were; they, too, were being watched, guarded, planned for. And this was what the human race really was, then, an insignificant breed of pets, kept in one of the minor hutches of the universe. When one of the pets tries to escape to another hutch a hand comes down to destroy it. And the pets must not know that there are other hutches, or that they have masters who are omnipotent. Oh, no! That would never do. They must be kept in ignorance for fear that they might upset the scheme of things, the pattern.

The priest, the king, the alien, and the man in the white coat gestured. "Shall we go into the other room?" he said.

CHAPTER EIGHT
Why? Why?

ON his way down in the elevator Wade changed his mind about going to Mars. He phoned Interplanetary and told them to have his plane ready the following morning, not immediately. Then he went back to his office, frowning.

There were a lot of things he didn't understand and going to Mars like a bullet from a gun wouldn't help him much. Waring would probably have come out from the Time Brain trance and might even have started back for Earth by the time he himself reached the Red Planet.

He needed time to think.

The office building was silent. Only in the Night Wing were the lights burning. Wade walked across his office and stood looking out of the crystal window. What was the key to all this mystery he wondered? There must be a key. There always had been before and invariably he had found it. But this time...

Now let us organize our facts, he mused. Let us line them up and look at them.

He lined up the facts and looked at them.

Van Carlsberg was in this somewhere. He had told him that he had found the fragment of the *Sunderling* when out near Titan. In actual fact Wade knew that he had not been near Titan, but had arrived from Mars. Therefore the Martians knew about the *Sunderling*. But the annoying thing was that he had a psycho recorder in his desk when Van Carlsberg had been telling him about his picking up the metal chunk and the thing hadn't reacted at all. No buzzing—no nothing. If the little spaceman had been lying it would have kicked up the most unholy din. Well, that could be explained. The Martians, if they were behind it, could have Installed false memory patterns, which would not affect the psycho recorder because so far as Van Carlsberg knew he would have been telling the truth. That might be the solution.

But that didn't explain the *reason* for it all. If the Marties wanted him to think that an Earthman had found the remains of the *Sunderling* that could mean only that they didn't want him to know that they had had anything to do with it. Again, why?

Martians didn't do things without reasons. That was certain. And to go to all this trouble they must have a very good reason. Presumably Yyrmac was in it as well and maybe more members of the Government and Science Council. It was difficult to think of any reason that they might have for such an intrigue and there was no way of finding out. If he got in touch with any of the Martians that he knew they wouldn't help him; Van Carlsberg was out because he must have had false memory patterns installed or else was a sufficiently good liar to defeat a psycho recorder! Failing these, the men who had told him that Van Carlsberg had been on Mars and had not been near Titan might all be liars and that was far from likely.

He looked at the facts and blinked. Before it had been a puzzle. Now it was something more. It was very unpleasant.

Outside the bright night signs of London blinked their messages at a sleeping world. A rocket came down with a roar to land, and above, twinkling like drops of dew, the stars. Wade glared up at them, his jaw jutting like a shelf. What was up there? Just a million million black circling worlds travelling round suns like and unlike Sol? Or was there life? Were there lands with green trees and rivers and white cities and fields? Were there people with big heads and spindly limbs? Were there silent blue men like the Martians with their spiders' legs or were there dwarfs living their lives beneath the soil as on Venus? Were there creatures with octopoid bodies and starfish eyes? Did they live in atmospheres of methane and ammonia vapor? Were their planets running with liquid hydrogen? How could he tell? And why, why, why had the *Sunderling* cracked up? He was not a spaceman, but he knew of the many ways a Ship could be destroyed in space, yet most of these accidents were the result of an imperfect ship. The *Sunderling* had been the most highly developed ship to leave Earth; it had had all the cosmic radiation protective screens, sensitive meteor spotters, the whole works. And it had smashed up somewhere in space.

He walked over to the far wall of his office and pressed a button. The wall slid away. A large screen was recessed there and beside it a double row of buttons stretching from knee level up to eye level. He located the right one and pressed.

There was a brief tangle of grid lines on the screen and a panorama of the London Spaceport came into focus. The *Sunderling* stood on the blast bay, surrounded by reporters, scientists, politicians, prominent people from all over Earth.

The day was brilliant, cloudless; a day in June.

There was Henessey talking to Sir Julian Smythills. And Nolan and McOrdle in conversation with a small crowd of reporters.

And there was Charles Talbot Wade, too, laughing with a crowd of scientists. Briefly he remembered the joke he had been telling them and smiled again. Over all of them the *Sunderling's* golden pencil reared towards the cloudless blue. Then there was a close-up of Henessey describing the superdrive in simple terms, telling also about the excellence of the ship itself, what an important day this was in the history of scientific achievement, or at any rate, research.

Wade pressed another button and the screen faded and blanked out. He did not want to watch the blasting off again.

He had run the film through eighteen times altogether since Van Carlsberg had brought the fragment of the *Sunderling* to the Newscreen building.

Charles Talbot Wade then started to pace the floor. He paced this way and that way, clockwise and anti-clockwise. He smoked cigars, he poured himself drinks, he downed cups of coffee, he picked objects off his desk and put them down again to resume his pacing.

He paced thus and so for twenty minutes.

The visor buzzed.

"Well?"

"Mr. Van Carlsberg, sir."

"In the flesh?"

"On the visor, sir."

"Put him through. "Why did those damned robots always look so cheerful? Someone ought to invent a robot that responded to your moods. When you were feeling serious they should look serious; when you were happy they should look happy, and so on…

Van Carlsberg's face looked like a pomegranate that had got old and rotten.

"Don't you sleep, either?" said Wade.

"Sometimes. Look, I've got something on my mind. Can I come and tell you about it?"

"About the *Sunderling?*"

"Yes."

"Come over right away, then. And brine your memory with you."

The wizened face grew astonished. "You guessed, then?"

"Yes, I guessed, and I've had a bit of information from people who say you hadn't been near Titan for over a year."

"I'm on my way to tell you about it."

P'rrrt went the visor and the screen blanked out.

Wade switched the psycho recorder on in his desk and lit another cigar. The smoke curled and settled in spirals on the desktop, then wisped away. So the memory patterns had been temporary ones. That meant that the Martians had only been concerned with making sure that no one knew *immediately* that they had discovered the fragment of the *Sunderling*. The fact that they had only installed temporary false memory patterns in Van Carlsberg proved that. And hadn't Van Carlsberg said, when first they discussed the piece of metal before Waring arrived. "If only we could travel back in time and see what happened to the ship—if only there was some *way.*" It had been cleverly done. It had remained for him to think of the Time Brain, as the Martians obviously knew he would. Very clever.

He did some more pacing, some more smoking, drank more cups of coffee. The smoke and the heat from the heater wall panels had made the room unbearably stuffy. He opened the crystal window, letting the coolness of the night enter like a welcomed guest. The sounds of the city picked holes in the silence; the humming of beetlecars, engines of the gyros. London never sleeps, he thought. There are always fools like me, up at crazy hours and envying the others who go to bed and sleep the long night through.

When Van Carlsberg arrived, Wade was still walking about the room.

"So you brought that lump of metal back from near Titan, did you?"

Van Carlsberg dropped into a chair and helped himself to coffee. "When I told you that I thought I was telling the truth."

"In actual fact you brought the thing over from Mars?"

"Yes."

"Well, why come and tell me about it now? Did the Martians pay you well for doing the job for them?"

"They didn't pay me anything at all. I only remembered being on Mars this evening, and I certainly don't recall ever accepting any bribes or commissions from them. My last re-collection of Mars was walking down besides the Central Canal."

No buzz from the psycho recorder. Wade grunted. "So they must have picked you up there, used hypnosis, and made you take the ship over to Earth with the lump of metal in it. Then when you landed on Earth you awoke to a set of false memories also supplied by our trusty Martian friends."

"What makes you think that?"

"Well, good God man, you were here telling me a long story about Titan and finding the *Sunderling* wreckage out there. Can't you remember that?

"Yes, I suppose I can." He put his head down between his hands and every part of him was shaking. He straightened. "I've been like this all evening. Can't seem to remember what's real and what I've dreamt. What did I tell you?"

"Simply that you'd been out near Titan and had come across this lump of the *Sunderling* floating about, had got it and brought it back to Earth. Sensing there might be a story in it and recognizing it as part of the *Sunderling* you brought it to me and hinted how wonderful it would be if we could travel back in time and see what had happened."

"I told you all that?"

"You surely did."

"Well."

"Well what? Can't you remember a thing?"

"It's all so muddled. I can't trust myself to say I remem-ber something that may just be one of the false memories. I remember being on Mars, walking along the Canal bank. It was dark, quiet. Stars out. A little wind coming in through the town. Then nothing. Not a thing more."

Wade poured another drink for the little quivering spaceman.

"Did you have any idea that there might be someone following you or watching you while you were in the town?"

"Now you mention it—perhaps. But you see, everything's all so confused. I may think someone had been following me simply because you just suggested it."

"Well, whether you remember it or not, that is what must have happened. You were watched, followed, and rendered unconscious. Then they gave you a strong dose of hypnosis, fitted you up with a set of false memories of where you'd been and what you'd done and told you to come and see me. They probably also suggested that you put the idea to me about going back in time to see what happened to the *Sunderling*."

"That's what it looks like, yes."

"Hmmm."

"Pardon?"

"Thinking."

A silence.

Then: "You know what all this looks like to me?"

Van Carlsberg shook his quivering head. "No—what?"

"It looks to me as though the Martians picked up the remains of the *Sunderling*, wanted us to find out what had happened to it, but didn't want to suggest we used the Time Brain. Does that sound sense?"

Van Carlsberg shrugged. "If you can think of a reason for them doing that, yes it does. But even so—why should they go to all the trouble of secrecy and hypnosis and so on? Why couldn't they have just delivered the remains to you and left it for you to ask if the Time Brain could be used?"

"First because if the Martians had officially found it the remains would have been delivered to the Earth Government, not to me, and second because I doubt very much whether all the high ups on Mars would approve of what's been done. As it is, they probably don't all know. If the thing had been done officially they *would* have known."

Van Carlsberg nodded. "You think, then, that there's some political reason behind all the secrecy. The right hand not letting the left hand know what it's doing?"

"I should say that's the case. The Martians are notoriously secretive about everything, but we do know that there's plenty of friction within their Government and Science Council. What is so galling is the fact that the Martians must know why the *Sunderling* never came back. Otherwise why should they take all this trouble?"

"If they know then, that may explain why no Martian ships have ever tried to reach the stars. I can't believe they have never come across the superdrive with all their science. In fact, I thought Henessey was supposed to have pinched some of his ideas from the Martians."

The two men stood silently, each thinking his own thoughts.

"It seems particularly strange to me," said Wade, after this silence, "that they should have let you revive and shake off the false memories so soon. They must have been pretty sure that I should, show interest and contact Mars straight away. And it also means that whatever plot they hatched is over now and they don't mind us knowing it. That's what's so odd, the fact that they don't mind us knowing."

The visor buzzed.

"Hullo? Wade here."

"Mr. Wade? Interplanetary relay call coming through via Martian ships *Dyyrpityg, GGryyl, Mnngyl.* Earth ships *Rameses, Manhattan, Reliance* and Satellite J.4 and Satellite J.3."

Wade breathed a great sigh of annoyance and impatience. "And Uncle Tom Cobley and all."

"Sorry, sir, orders state that we must inform the party called of all stations relaying an interplanetary call and—"

"Yes, yes. Who's the call from?"

"—on no account must these regulations be disregarded. Interplanetary calls cost several thousand credits per minute." The plastic and rubberoid smile flashed briefly apologetically. "Your call is from Central Repair Laboratory, Cyylg Province, Mars. Your caller is a Mr. Yyrmac. I am putting you through now."

Wade made a sign to Van Carlsberg, who turned up the amplifier so that he could listen in to the conversation. "It's Yyrmac, calling from Mars. Costing him thousands," breathed Wade. Van Carlsberg nodded. "It's a pity someone doesn't think up a way of relaying visor pictures across space. I'd like to see Yyrmac when he's talking to me. It's amazing the way you can tell when someone's got something to hide—even a Martian."

A noise like a thousand grasshoppers scraping their legs came into the room from the amplifier. Gradually a deeper, harsher crackling took over. There was a period of harsh pops and then the high, brittle voice of the Martian came through. His voice was as brittle as his spidery legs, thought Wade, listening.

"Wade? Your man Waring has finished his adventure."

"How is he? What happened?"

"Oh, we don't know yet. After a spell as long as this we let them sleep off the effects. He'll be more or less uncon-scious for several days. I'd like you to be here when he wakes if you can manage it."

"You want me there?"

"Yes. There are a number of things that I feel we ought to talk about."

"How right you are. A number of things."

"If you take a plane to your Satellite J.3 a Martian ship will pick you up there."

"Right. By the way—can I bring Van Carlsberg with me?"

"Who's he? Yes, if you want to—is he one of your men?"

"I thought he was one of yours."

"I don't know what you're talking about. But bring him if you wish. Goodbye."

The scrapings, crackling and poppings took over. Then silence once more. Wade switched off and straightened. "You want to come?" he asked. Van Carlsberg nodded vigorously. "Perhaps they'll tell me what they did with a week or so of my life," he grated.

Wade visored through once more to the field and told them to get his plane ready immediately. Then the two men left Newscreen together, taking Wade's beetlecar.

At the port the small private rocket glittered in the starlight.

"Satellite J.3," Wade informed the pilot, then he and Van Carlsberg had a drink at the all-night bar while the pilot mapped course and set his instruments. They sat at a small table drinking. The bar was quiet, a few spacemen swilling beer in a corner. It was four in the morning.

"So we're going to find out what's what, are we?" said Van Carlsberg.

"That's what it looks like. Yyrmac must have relented and decided to tell all."

"Unless the need for secrecy is over. He said Waring had come out of the Time Brain thing. Perhaps they were only concerned with getting him there and sending him back in time. Once that was done, there might be no further need for keeping things dark."

"You could be right. There's the pilot. We're ready to go."

They went.

The rocket blasted off in a shiver of red flame and noise like tearing calico, taking them out to where Satellite J.3 circled Earth.

And on the journey they sat silently, feeling that at last the mystery was going to be solved, though in what way they had no idea. It seemed ridiculous that the Martians should now be prepared to discuss openly a matter that they had taken such great pains to hide.

The rocket moved in space like a silver humming-bird trailing a streamer of vermilion fire behind it.

It reached the satellite and then there was a commotion and a bustle as the electro-magnetic grab corridor swung out like a section of a giant snake, coupling onto the airlock. Wade and Van Carlsberg went up into the satellite.

A spaceman, recognizing Van Carlsberg, saluted.

"Good morning to you. We're expecting to be picked up by a Martian ship."

"Yes, sir, she's radioed through and coming in now. You timed it very well."

The Martian ship was big and fast and within minutes it was alongside. They watched it through the giant windows of the satellite, a giant red bulk against the blackness. The corridor snaked once more, coupling with the airlock. One of the satellite officials opened the door of the airlock to welcome a blue spidery Martian.

"Mr. Wade?"

"That's right."

"We are to take you to Mars." He consulted golden sheets of papery metal. They rustled and clicked in his blue fingers. "These instructions mention *one* Earthman—" He looked questioningly at Van Carlsberg.

"Van Carlsberg is one of my men," said Wade.

"I am sorry, Mr. Wade. I can only take you."

"Look, I have had a relay call from Yyrmac at the Repair Laboratory. He said it would be quite in order for me to bring Van Carlsberg with me."

The Martian moved his brittle legs about and consulted his gold sheets once again. "Well," he said. "There's nothing here to say anything about that."

"Naturally not. You'd left Mars before Yyrmac got through to me. I'll answer any questions and take full responsibility when we reach Mars."

That seemed to satisfy the Martian. He nodded and Wade and Van Carlsberg followed him up out into the Martian ship.

Sponge seats had been fitted inside the ship, showing that it was normally used for transporting Earthmen, the Martians never needing such additional comforts.

There was a *whooshing*. The red ship speeded towards its home planet, leaving the satellite a bright disc growing ever smaller behind it.

CHAPTER NINE
The Last Answer

"I T seems so stupid, so useless."

"I suppose it must do."

"So purposeless and unfair."

"But there *is* a purpose, and to the rest of the universe it is far from unfair."

The five of them were talking in the room, Rumbold, Nolan, Henessey, McOrdle and the Guardian, the being brought to life by their own fancies, the minion of the Planners. And the four spoke, all of them, knowing that soon they would be no more. Dust they might become, perhaps; dust to float through the black voids without end in meaningless patterns until eventually they might get drawn down into a sun or onto a world, or they might forever float from dark behind to dark before, never touching anything. Never.

Nolan found himself wondering who would have gone on the trip if he had not. Mitchell, perhaps, or Van Carlsberg. And then it would have been they who would have had to have faced this death a million miles and a million years from Earth, from sanity, from cold, clear, clean three-dimensional logic. And he himself might have taken a ship to Venus and at this very moment he might have been breathing the moist atmosphere of the Twilight Zone, or driving through the blistered desert of the Sun Side, seeing the volcanoes popping their gouts of crimson lava. Or he might have been on Mars, even, walking where the canals gleamed their silver smiles under the moons. Any of these places he might have been. Any of them.

But he was not there. He was *here*. And here was nowhere.

Sometimes long ago when he had first been into space he had felt that he was nowhere. But never so much as now. Now he was nowhere and there was no getting away from it. And suddenly he felt a terrible longing for Earth, such as he had not known for years. It was a longing that came to him as a gripping pain in his throat, in his heart, everywhere all at once. He thought of fields and trees and all good, green things. And in his thoughts were cool rivers, where he had swum as a boy, and there was a red brick school and houses, with smoke curling up from chimneys. There were windows brightly glowing on winter evenings and there were warm, cozy pubs; all things like these crowding each other in his mind. All tumbling in a shimmering mass through his thoughts, to become wisps of dreams and float away before he could hold them down and savor them to the full.

And the thought that was strongest in his mind, despite all these memories, was: *There is nothing I can do, nothing at all.* There was nothing anyone could do against the Planners. He was sure of that.

Briefly he remembered Henessey's interview with him prior to the trip.

"We need someone who *knows* about space and who knows about dealing with alien life forms we may encounter. I don't mean laboratory experience, I mean real experience. We think you're the man for the job."

How *pleased* he had felt, hearing Henessey say that. And what good had the qualities been to him? No good whatsoever. Certainly he *knew* about space, certainly, too, he *knew* about dealing with alien life forms. He had been on Venus and Mars. But just because he *knew* about these things he had felt entitled to go with them on the *Sunderling*. How foolish, how *mad!* It needed more than a spaceman to deal with the fourth dimension and the Planners.

He felt resentful that he should have to die for a reason he did not fully understand. There seemed no justice in it, and in spite of the fact that he had travelled throughout most of the Solar System, he still retained a vague belief in justice. Anger came up within him in a red, raw wave. It battered at every memory of the past and fastened its teeth on the hideous present.

Nolan had to make an effort to prevent himself from striking out at the alien, tentacled thing in front of him. And the absurdity of that, too, struck him. What good would it do to strike a thing that wasn't really there at all? But nevertheless it posed a question. Would his fist sink *through* it, or would he encounter hard, tangible flesh and bone? He was sorely tempted. His hands itched with small itches at his sides where they were hanging, now limp, now tense. His mouth moved and he felt his neck grow hot, then cold. Then his body slackened.

He felt suddenly so very old. His body dropped all of its overt tenseness and his muscles ran to jelly within him. There wasn't any use in hitting out and he knew it. And the thing, watching him with its three multiple eyes, knew that he knew it.

McOrdle felt no anger, only resignation. He knew that what the man in the golden robe had told him was true. Man was unfitted to go out into space and explore worlds different from his own. He was not an adult creature capable of dealing with all manner of different life forms and situations; rather was he the adolescent that this being described. And how utterly unaware of his adolescence man was! McOrdle laughed to himself when he thought of all the high-ups in the political and scientific fields who imagined themselves so superior, so grand in their own little worlds. He thought of them as the Planners must see them—as nothing more than a handful of insignificant creatures fairly low on the evolutionary scale, but dangerous if allowed to roam too far. And it applied equally to all men, past and present. Columbus, Newton, Farraday, Genghis Khan, Marco Polo, Julius Caesar, Barbarossa, all of them. Nothing but a crowd of dangerous adolescents who had to be watched as a nanny watches her little charges.

And the trouble was that it was quite right that the Planners should watch. Quite right. If they had the welfare of the universe at heart, then it was only just that they should watch humanity and prevent it from spawning its evil on other worlds.

He turned to say something to Rumbold and noticed an odd glare in the psychologist's eyes.

"Let's pray and we shall be saved," shouted Rumbold.

"What's that? What did you say?" Amazed, the men clustered round.

Rumbold dropped on his knees on the floor. "Praise God and we'll be saved. Praise God. Pray to Him, all of you; pray and we'll be saved from death. And we'll return to Earth and tell them that they must destroy all their space ships and all their machines. We'll tell them that they must turn about and go backwards to the days when men believed. Then they'll be saved, too. Down on your knees, down, down..."

The men looked at each other, lifting their eyebrows, making gestures as though to still the foaming words.

Rumbold clasped his hands in prayer. "Come, join me, brethren," he said. The men shifted their feet and looked out of place. The spectacle of a man going mad was not new to them, but here on this strange world it seemed so absurd, so useless.

McOrdle bent down, taking the psychologist by the shoulder, gripping. "It's all right, old fellow. It's all right. Everything's going to be fine."

"Yes, yes, I know. Down on your knees, down on your knees beside me and we will pray together and we will be saved." Tears were running down Rumbold's plump face. McOrdle suddenly wanted to laugh. It was all too absurd.

Rumbold started to say the Lord's Prayer.

"What are we going to do with him?" Nolan asked the alien creature.

"He will come round in a second or so."

"...which art in Heaven..."

"But are you *sure* he will?"

"I am quite sure. There is nothing I can do. I cannot alter the way a man's mind works."

"It's terrible. I suppose you're proud to have reduced him to this?"

"Proud? Of course not."

"...give us this day our daily bread..."

"Then I suppose the Planners are proud. They must get something out of doing things like this."

"The Planners feel sorrow that such things are necessary. But they know that they are necessary."

Nolan laughed a short, harsh laugh. "What do you mean, they feel sorrow? How can a non-human creature experience a human emotion?"

The alien was silent for a moment. Then it said, "It is difficult for me to answer that question. The Planners are made in such a way that they *do* experience sorrow and other emotions. But they experience them only slightly. If they experienced them in any degree of strength they would not be able to function as Planners."

"...forever and ever. Amen."

The men looked at Rumbold. He was kneeling with his hands clasped together In front of him. Tears had run on his face and dropped onto his shirt. He looked at each of them in turn and then looked at the priest. There was no sign of recognition in his eyes. They were little orbs of hate and danger burning in his face. He scrambled to his feet, chuckled once, and ran for the door. McOrdle lunged to catch him, but a heavy blow from the back of Rumbold's hand knocked him to the floor. The door banged. Rumbold was gone.

Henessey laughed. "I tried that. It didn't work."

The being shook its head. "No, it never does work."

Another door opened. Rumbold stumbled through and fell, breathless.

"Why don't you kill him now?" said Nolan, his voice rising. "Why hang on like this? You can kill us all and have done with it. What's the sense in us being here, just standing about going crazy? Let's get it over with."

Rumbold laughed and rolled about on the floor. Then he went into a corner and started to recite the Lord's Prayer once more.

"Nolan's right," said McOrdle. "Get it done. You intend to kill us, I presume?"

The man in the gold robe sighed. "I intend nothing. The Planners have decreed that you must die. It is the only way. Perhaps you are thinking that. I could blot out your memory of all that has happened and send you back in your ship to Earth? No, that would not work out. There would be questions that you would not be able to answer about your reasons for returning. Nor can I transport you to another planet similar to Earth. There would probably be life on it or at any rate on another planet in the same system. Then there would be the chance that the other creatures would wonder where you came from, what you were. Even if I removed knowledge of the Planners from your mind, the other creatures might suspect *something*. And that must not happen."

"In other words—we're dead men," said McOrdle.

"That is truer than you imagine."

"What do you mean by *that?*"

"Just what I say. You and your ship ate no more than dust and fragments at this very moment. You exist here in another dimension, don't forget."

"Why did you bring us here in the first place? You knew we had to die. Why did you have to bring us here?"

"So that you should see. So that you should know."

"So that we should understand why we have to die? Or rather why we died?"

"Yes."

"Very considerate of you. Yes, very considerate I must say."

"There is no sense in being bitter. What has to be has to be and that is the end of it. There is no other way."

Henessey looked at the man in the white coat. "May I have a word? Thank you. I wanted to ask whether we could all go back to the ship. The fourth dimensional ship, I mean. Presumably the one we built and manned is floating round the cosmos in little pieces at this moment."

The man in the white coat smiled thinly, tiredly. "Yes, it is. You may return to the ship if you wish."

Nolan and McOrdle looked at Henessey and nodded. Rumbold crooned a prayer to himself, gazing at the others with eyes that shone wildly—an idiot's eyes.

"We'd better take Rumbold with us," said McOrdle, softly.

"Where? Where?" said Rumbold. "Where are you taking me? And who are you to decide where I shall go and what I shall do?"

Nolan and McOrdle stepped up to Rumbold quickly. The psychologist was on his feet in an instant, glaring at them, his fingers curled into claws and his breath coming in brief little gasps between his teeth.

"You shall not take me. I have prayed and I am safe. I shall go back to Earth and teach them how *they* can be saved. I shall break the machines and cast the moneylenders from the temple. Listen." He raised a shaking hand to his ear. "Listen—it is the voice of the Lord that I hear, and the singing of angels is in my ears."

Nolan looked questioningly about him. Henessey was staring fixedly at the psychologist and McOrdle also. There was only one thing to do, thought Nolan. He hit Rumbold a great blow on the side of his head. Rumbold gave a dull, moaning cry and fell.

"It was the only thing I could do," said Nolan.

The others nodded.

Then Nolan hefted Rumbold onto his shoulder. "The ship?" he asked.

They went out of the building, then, all of them. Nolan carrying Rumbold on his shoulder, the being walked slightly in front of them. And when they got outside the building and looked back there was no building there, only a black plane, and the blackness of space above it.

"I knew that would happen," said McOrdle, looking over his shoulder.

Nolan did not turn round. "The building's gone, hasn't it?" he asked.

"Yes. Nothing there now. Nothing left."

"Its purpose is served," said the man in the gold robes to McOrdle.

"But it will have to be used again, eventually," said Henessey.

"What do you mean?"

"Man isn't going to stop trying to reach the stars solely because we don't come back. He'll go on trying. He'll try forever, don't you see that?"

The man in the white coat nodded. "Yes, I see it. But eventually man may develop sufficiently for the Planners to allow him to succeed in his quest."

Henessey looked up quickly. "You really think that?"

"The Planners think it is possible. There are patterns in the future that tell of man's maturity. There are also those which tell of his death."

"Which are the true patterns?"

"That remains to be seen. The Planners will not guide man on to intellectual maturity, nor will they prevent him from attaining such a state. They are there only to watch his progress."

"But have the Planners no views as to what will happen?" Henessey was excited now.

"The Planners know the possibilities."

"Yes, yes. But have they no *feelings* about the thing? They have watched the development of life on Earth and on all the other planets as well. Have they made no comparisons? Is humanity backward, considering the time it has taken to get up out of the mud? Can the Planners not tell through their experience of other planets and the life forms on them? Can't they see what is likely to happen on Earth?"

"Yes. They can see what is likely to happen."

"Well, then?"

"It is not pleasant."

"What is not pleasant? The future of humanity?"

"Yes."

"Tell me."

"It will not do you any good to die with it in your mind."

"Tell me."

"The Planners have watched humanity's progress as they have watched the progress of many other parallel races on other worlds. The indications are that Earth will destroy itself within three centuries at least. It may be sooner."

Henessey heard the words that he knew he would hear, heard the views of those who had watched countless other races rise and fall. He felt he had known all along.

"The ship," said McOrdle.

And there it was. The ship. Just as it had been when they stepped out of it. But they knew now that it was but a shadow, a fourth dimensional ghost installed there to gratify their last wish.

They trudged over the plain and came up to it. The silvery sheen of its metal seemed real enough. Nolan reached out with his free hand and touched the hull. Solid.

"Here we are," said McOrdle.

"Yes, here we are," said Nolan, lowering Rumbold to the ground. The psychologist stirred and sat up, pawing the black ground with his pudgy hands. "The Lord's name be praised," he said.

"It's all right, Rumbold," said McOrdle, softly. "We're going back to Earth."

"To Earth? Back to Earth?"

"That's right. Back home again."

"I shall preach in the market places. I shall tell all the people that they must mend their ways, that they must *believe* again. The people must know, they must be told that they are going wrong and they must be led, like little children they must be led." _

Henessey spoke softly to the man in the white coat. "Can we get into the ship before you—before it happens? Can we get Rumbold into the ship so that he thinks he's going back home again?"

"You can if you wish."

Henessey turned to the others. "Right men. Into the ship."

Rumbold raised his eyes to the blackness above. "Home," he said. "I'm going home to spread the Word of the Lord throughout all the lands of the Earth." He started up the ladder with the others behind him.

After taking a few steps, Henessey, the last, turned and descended again. He looked at the man in the white coat.

"Tell me," he said. "Is there any way of knowing what the Planners look like? Can you show me one?"

"You will wish that you had not seen."

"I want to see. If I'm to die then I want to see."

"It will not benefit you."

"Show me, can't you?"

"Watch me closely."

The man in the white coat, stood quite still and slowly Henessey noticed that his form was changing. There was a wavering about the lines of his face. The white coat darkened, brightened, dulled. A strange iridescence came over the figure and it grew until there seemed but a glowing oval of brightness where before a man had stood. Henessey peered closer and then he saw the thing taking form. He watched as metallic sheens started to appear and gleaming bulbs of eyes and wire-like antennae.

The thing stood there before him—a robot.

Henessey turned away and started up the ladder. His mind seemed only half-awake, the rest of it dulled by what he had seen. A robot. Who, then, had planned the Planners? He went in through the airlock and Nolan drew up the long ladder. The great door of the *Sunderling* closed.

And that was the end.

In the three normal, known dimensions the interstellar ship *Sunderling* exploded. There was a red burst of flame and a light that flashed in eternal darkness among the stars.

There was a tearing as great metal slabs were torn apart and flung wide into darkness. A great hand pushed outwards on every part of the ship, tearing walls and floors, machines and instruments with terrible force.

And the force exploded within the men, too. Within each of them at the same moment, so that parts of exploded men stuck to parts of the ship as it flared and expanded in all its jigsaw pieces to trail endlessly through space.

But one piece of the ship there was that did not trail endlessly. It went its separate way through the black midnights like a silver bullet, speeding. And such was the force of the explosion and the speed of the hurtling fragment, and the direction of the fragment, that, wonder upon wonders, it was picked up.

A Martian ship retrieved it from its travels and brought it back to Mars, where Martian scientists recognized it for what it was and told their Government. The Martian Government, knowing what must have happened to the ship and realizing that they could turn the recovery of this fragment to some useful purpose, conceived a plan. They acquired an Earthman, who, under hypnosis, took the fragment back to Earth and showed it to Charles Talbot Wade. Wade obtained permission to use the Time Brain and sent his reporter, Waring, with the fragment to Mars. There the fragment was attached to the Brain and Waring went back into time...

A thousand star shells burst about Waring's head. A blackness that might have been a very dark redness crept all over him.

One Waring floated in space, the other Waring sat in a strange chair with a helmet on his head.

Slowly the Warings merged into one.

Waring slept.

CHAPTER TEN
Explanation

"So you know nothing?"

"I'm sorry, Mr. Wade. We have instructions to tell nothing. When we reach Mars I am assured that all your questions will be answered. At present—there is nothing I can say."

Wade lapsed into silence, chewing on the end of his cigar. He snuggled further into the sponge rubber seat next to Van Carlsberg and scowled. Still all his questions were unanswered. Still he didn't know why all the secrecy had been felt necessary.

The big Martian ship gnawed through the darkness, effortless and smooth in its passage. It came down through the long night of space, passing near one of the glowing Martian moons, down, down into the thin atmosphere of the planet.

"You're landing at the Repair Laboratory, I take it?" asked Wade.

"No. We are landing at Rrngyl first. There are a number of Government officials who are waiting there to see you."

"Government officials?"

"Yes."

"But why? I understood that r was being taken to see Yyrmac at the Repair Laboratory. Why do I have to see Government officials?"

"I am sorry, Mr. Wade, but I cannot answer your questions. I am only acting under instructions from my Government."

"In other words, I've been kidnapped." Wade scowled more fiercely. The Martian turned his blue head away and looked out at the bright Martian day.

"Have you been to our planet many times, Mr. Wade?" he said.

"Uh-huh," said Wade.

"You like it?"

"Hmmm," said Wade.

The Martian gave up. Seven minutes later they landed.

They walked down the ramp onto the bright concrete of the spaceport. The sky was blue about them and the buildings tau and white and very tine. Wade glowered.

From the other side of the wide concrete stretch a small party of Martians emerged from a building and started to walk towards the rocket. Wade could tell they were Government men by the red and grey coloring of their dress.

"Damned spiders," said Van Carlsberg beside him, under his breath.

"What this all means I really don't know," said Wade, in exasperation. "We were originally going to be taken to Yyr-mac and now we've got to talk to these people. The more I try and sort the tangle out the more involved it all becomes. You'd better let me do the talking."

The Martians came up to them. One of them gave the Martian ceremonial salute and then extended his hand. Wade shook it and then stood back, waiting.

"We are very glad to see you, Mr. Wade. I imagine that you are wondering what this is all about."

"I certainly am."

"I hope we shall be able to enlighten you. If you will come with us, please?"

They had no alternative. The little party set off for the main road, where a car waited.

"I must say I think you have been extremely high-handed. I was supposed to be visiting Yyrmac at the Central Repair Laboratory and the pilot of your ship brought me here. I had no idea what I was being brought here for and no one would tell me. My Government will hardly view such behavior lightly when I tell them."

The leading Martian nodded. "I can quite understand how you must feel. I can only say that when you have heard our reasons for acting in this seemingly peculiar way, you will agree that we were justified in doing so. Incidentally, we are going to Vvaron Building."

They reached the golden car, Wade turned. "Vvaron Building? Then your President—?"

"Yes. It is President NNomar who wishes to speak to you. I fear that this entire matter is rather more important both to Mars and to Earth for it to be dealt with through the normal channels."

A rocket roared over drowning further conversation. They got into the golden car and were whisked away down the broad, white, gleaming road to the far end of the city.

Inside the car, Wade looked out of the window, his mind buzzing with the things he had learned. So the Martian President was concerned now was he? The thing got more and more complex. Wade knew full well that the Martian President left most of the Government work to others under normal circumstances. Therefore this must be something very special. Beside him, Van Carlsberg quivered and shook.

The golden car sped along the roads between the towers of tall and stately buildings. It sped past gardens and parks, past low, single-storey buildings, and past minarets of crystal and ancient stone. It moved like a silent bubble along beside the wide and glittering silver of the canal, where the emerald ships sailed as they had sailed the past ten thousand years, gleaming like green-jeweled swans upon the waters.

And, like Waring before him, Wade felt the age of Mars press on him from every side. He felt, too, that he knew more about that strange feeling of antiquity than he had before. The Martians already knew so much more than the men of Earth. They were entitled to their air of knowledge and settledness.

The car swung past a long white wall and entered a garden. At the far end of a long silver road a building nestled among trees. Through the open windows of the car the small breezes blew smells of flowers and growing things. The strange, ethereal music of Martian pipes came from all parts of the garden, where robot players piped summer and winter, day and night, their music filling the air and the lungs, filling the mind and the body. It was a strange music and though Wade had heard it before here on Mars it had never affected him quite so strongly in the past. Now it seemed to symbolize all the mystery of Mars and the Martian peoples with their oddly serene expressions and their secrecy. As though they knew all the secrets of the universe and weren't saying anything about them to anyone, no matter what. Wade found that the car had stopped and the door was being held open for him.

He stepped out. The air was cool and fresh about him, fragrant with the spicy smell of artificial plants lining the walls of the building.

"This way, please." The Martians led him up to the building and, together, they all entered.

Four new Martians whispered forward on brittle legs. "Mr. Wade? With us, if you will," said one, motioning with his hand.

They went into a circular elevator and ascended to the top of the building. Through luminous corridors, then, towards a vast blue door, with the Imperial Martian Crest set in its centre. The door opened for them and they went inside to meet President NNomar.

The Martians bowed low.

Wade stood where he was, with Van Carlsberg slightly behind him.

"Please enter and sit down, Mr. Wade. Ah! Van Carlsberg, I believe. Though you will not remember it we have met before. Please sit down both of you."

They sat down facing the President on long, low, sponge-rubber chairs.

The President looked just the same as all the other Martians. Spidery and blue, with liquid silver eyes that rolled and expanded, settled, contracted, flared and dulled, all in turn.

"I have no doubt that your minds are full of questions. I have given instructions to my men that you were not to be told anything until I · had seen you. I admit that this may seem very officious and discourteous, but I can assure you I gave those instructions for an excellent reason.

There was a rustling. The President produced a sheaf of golden papery sheets and handed them to Wade. "That will give you the story of everything we have been doing, but I will summarize it briefly for you to save time.

"Firstly, we knew about your attempt to reach the stars in your ship, the *Sunderling*. We knew that you had discovered the principle of what you term the superdrive and had applied it to this ship, thus making faster-than-light speeds possible. About eighteen months after the *Sunderling* had set off, one of our ships picked up a fragment of an Earth ship. We made investigations and found that it was part of your interstellar ship."

"I thought that was what had happened," said Wade.

"Yes. Well, we were anxious, for reasons that I will detail later, that you should know that the *Sunderling* had broken up in space. We were also anxious that you should try and find out what had caused it to break up. The Time Brain is the only machine in our System capable of finding out what has happened in the past and we wanted you to use that. Had we told you all this we should have had to tell your Government and they would have had to have applied for official permission from our Government to use the Time Brain for such a purpose. That much is plain, I think?"

"Certainly."

"Good. Now, the Governmental system of this planet works on roughly democratic lines, as you know, and there would have been a very good chance that permission to use the Brain would have been refused. I did not want that to happen. I wanted you to use the Brain and find out what *did* occur in space to smash up your first interstellar ship. I wanted you to know for many reasons, but they can wait. In order to do this I had to make it appear as if you yourself thought of the idea of going back into time. I found that Van Carlsberg was on Mars and arranged for him to be brought here—"

"Unconscious," put in Van Carlsberg.

"Unconscious, yes," nodded the President. "Once here I installed false memory patterns in him and sent him back to your planet with the fragment of the *Sunderling*. From that point I take it you know the story."

"Of course."

"Van Carlsberg was instructed to plant the idea of time travel in your mind. We knew that your only deep personal contact among the more prominent people on Mars was Yyrmac, so we informed Yyrmac that if were to contact him he was to help you in any way he could to use the Time Brain. There again the Time Brain could not be used *officially* for such a purpose; if it had been, some members of the Science Council would have asked the Government where the authority came from. Naturally I did not want that to happen. So Yyrmac had the Brain moved to the Repair Laboratory and there your man Waring was taken when he landed. And there he has travelled back through time and seen the fate of the *Sunderling*."

Wade nodded. "Well, all that seems clear, as far as it goes. But What I cannot understand is why you have done all this? I can understand some of the reasons for your secrecy, but not all. Why did you want us to know what had happened to our ship in the first place? And why did you think that the Government, if approached officially, would refuse permission to use the Time Brain—was it because of the nature of what we intended to find out?"

The President smiled. "I imagined you would ask those questions. I think it would really be best if you were to wait until your man Waring has told his story. Then you will see why the Government would probably have refused permission. As for your first question—why did I feel you should know? Well, that, too, would be better answered when you have heard Waring's story. I am sorry to have to keep you in suspense like this, Mr. Wade, but I feel it is for the best."

Wade shrugged. There was nothing he could do. "Just as you say," he said.

Van Carlsberg leaned forward, his face twitching, nests of wrinkles appearing and disappearing round his eyes and mouth. "Tell me, sir," he said, "what did you do to me? I remember walking along beside a canal and then—nothing."

One of the other Martians standing respectfully aside spoke up. "We had been watching you for some time. Did you ever wonder *why* you were walking along beside the canal?"

Van Carlsberg looked at him. His eyes clouded as he tried to think back, to remember. "No, no. I can't seem to recall where I was going or anything. The whole business is so confused—"

The Martian smiled. "You had been under long-range hypnosis for several days; we drew you to that spot near the canal and then put you under deep hypnosis, installing the false memories at the same time."

Van Carlsberg grunted, but said nothing.

"I must say I think your reasons had better be good ones for doing all this," said Wade. "It's unethical and high-handed in the extreme, and I can't see my Government taking a very pleasant view of it."

The President's face was grave. "It isn't normal Martian practice to act in this way I can assure you. But there are occasions when exceptional steps are necessary to deal with exceptional circumstances."

On the wall a screen glowed, winking redly. One of the Martians stepped over to it, pressed a button, and commenced to speak in Martian. After a few moments of animated conversation he snapped the screen off and turned to the President. "Yyrmac says the Earthman is due to awaken in about an hour, sir."

The President stood up. "Shall we go, gentlemen?"

The journey to the Central Repair Laboratory they made in a long golden car belonging to the President. It swept its way along the winding roads out of the towns until all the silver spires and glinting crystal minarets were behind them, fading into misty distances.

The red mountains of Mars projected their teeth at the brilliant sky and the golden sand shifted with the winds that blew.

It was not a long journey. The sleek golden car gobbled the roads and if gobbled the minutes that the journey took. Soon they were climbing higher into the mountains, and

Wade, gazing out of the window, looked Gown across the great plain that stretched away to the towns beyond. There were the canals, glittering as always, and there the spires of the city they had just left. The sun, far away, remote, gleamed redly above the horizon, and Wade could see a dust storm whirling like a small spiral of darkness way off beyond, the next mountain range.

"Here we are," said one of the Martians.

Inside the Laboratory, Yyrmac met them, bowing before the President, smiling at Wade. They went into the main laboratory and Wade started. There was the Time Brain, set against the wall. Beside it, lying on a couch, his eyes closed, was Waring.

Yyrmac walked up to Wade. "I imagine you have been told most of the story," he said.

"Well, I've been told *what* has been done, but not *why*."

"No, I don't know half the reasons myself. In fact, I'm almost as much in the dark as you are. I was approached by one of the Government men and told to expect a call from you requesting permission to use the Time Brain. When I received the call I was to offer any reasonable help. Just why the President wanted you to know what happened to your interstellar ship I don't know."

Wade looked at the Martian quickly. "But you know what happened to the ship, don't you?"

"Yes."

"Well then, what *did* happen?"

The President's voice cut in to their conversation. "I was telling Mr. Wade that he had better hear the story from his own man first. Then we can discuss reasons and so on afterwards. That seems to me the best arrangement."

Yyrmac nodded. "Very well, sir," he said. "The Earthman should be waking very shortly."

"How many of the Science Council know that this has been going on?" said Wade to Yyrmac in a low voice.

"Only a few. I know most of the heads of the departments in this place and they are only aware that the Brain is being used by Earthmen. They do not know the purpose to which it is being put. I arranged for the Brain to be moved here from the other Laboratory as soon as I received your message telling me that you wanted to use it. At the Main Laboratory I only know a few of the scientists and some of them might have suspected things; they would certainly have asked questions."

The group had gathered about the couch where Waring slept, his chest rising and falling with the motion of his breathing.

What has he seen? thought Wade. What *is* behind all this, and why do the Martians want us to know? Or rather why do some of them want us to know?

The eternal questions buzzed in his head as they had buzzed since first Van Carlsberg had told him about finding the fragment of the *Sunderling*. They were a part of him now, never letting go of his mind for the briefest of moments even. Always they were there to bite and nibble at his thoughts.

"Look," said Van Carlsberg, suddenly.

Silence came among them.

The only noise was the hum of the generators.

"He's waking," said the President.

CHAPTER ELEVEN
What the Martians Knew

WARING slept. His body was quite still, save for the gentle rise and fall of his chest. His face portrayed nothing of what he had seen and experienced.

He slept. And while he slept he dreamed.

He was back once again on the *Sunderling*, and he was within each of the men in turn. He could see with their eyes, breathe with their noses, hear with their ears, and think with their minds. He was Rumbold when he stepped out of the spaceship and started down the long ladder onto the black asteroid. He was Rumbold, too, afterwards, crying the praises of God to a black sky and a circle of oddly unfamiliar faces. Who were these people? He didn't know them. He'd never seen them before. *He* was saved, but they were not. He found he was saying the Lord's Prayer.

Then he was Nolan, trying to imagine what the occupant of the asteroid would look like and he was Nolan when Nolan was wishing he had never come, wishing he had been on Venus or Mars or out in space riding the mighty dark in a ship he knew how to handle.

Then he was Henessey running through the endless grey corridors of the building, pausing here for breath, there to see if anyone was giving chase. Henessey running in terror to escape from a building that he had only just recognized as existing at all, and only just seen for what it was—a lunatic asylum.

The images of the men were jumbled together now, in Waring's dream. He was Rumbold and Henessey together, and Nolan and McOrdle together, and then Rumbold and

Nolan, and then Henessey and McOrdle. Then he was only a part of each of them. His mind, then, became four tiny pieces of mind, each one containing a part of the men.

And over everything there was that *thing* that they all had seen in different forms. As Nolan he had seen it as a strange, alien creature, as Rumbold—a priest, as McOrdle—a man in a golden robe, and as Henessey he had seen it as a man in a white coat. But now it was different, now it was just a wispy, shadowy thing that hovered everywhere. Everywhere, all at once, it was. Its outlines were vague, shimmering. It glistened in a light that came from nowhere and went nowhere with no purpose in its coming or its going.

Waring turned slightly on the couch.

In his dream the thing was changing shape, becoming that strange oval of light that Henessey had seen. And within the oval the Planner's face stared out metallically, stolidly, expressionlessly. A metallic face. A *robot.*

Waring screamed twice and sat up on the couch, sweating.

They clustered round him. Wade was putting his hand on his shoulder. "It's all right now, old man. It's over, all over."

"Where—what—?" He slumped back on the couch, holding his hands over his face.

Wade looked up at the Martians savagely. "What did he see—?" he demanded. "What did he see to make him scream?"

"He's been asleep for some time. A coma. Possibly he had a dream while he was waking."

"I'm okay now," said Waring on the couch.

A Martian brought something over in a glass and made him drink it down. After a few minutes the reporter shook his head and smiled weakly.

"Feel up to talking?" asked Wade, his voice quick, nervous.

"Yes, I'll talk." He gave a startled gasp as he recognized the uniform of some of the Martian Government men and the Imperial Crest on the President's tunic.

"It's all right, Waring old man. Go ahead and talk. I'll explain everything else later," said Wade, gesturing at the assembled Martians.

So Waring talked. He told everything he had been through. He described it all in detail, even including the dream.

Listening to him Wade's face grew paler and paler, as did that of Van Carlsberg. Incredulity, surprise, horror—it was on all there on their faces as they listened to the story of what had happened to the *Sunderling*.

The rose glow had faded from the sky and the two moons had risen out of the twilight to saunter like lost ghosts in the sky by the time Waring had finished telling his tale.

The darkness of a Martian night had fallen outside and those within the laboratory could look up out of the crystal glass roof and see the stars shining brightly, brightly…

But Wade sat on the foot of the couch with his face buried in his hands. Van Carlsberg stared from Wade to Waring and then to the Martians. The tale was over.

"It *can't* be true," whispered Wade.

"The Time Brain is incapable of lies," said the President, gently.

"It's true," said Waring, his voice tired, dull. "I know that it's true in the same way that Henessey knew it, and Rumbold and Nolan and McOrdle. It's all true. Every bit of it."

"But everything we've believed in—" said Van Carlsberg.

"What have we believed in? *Ourselves,* that's all we've ever believed in for the last century."

Wade did not look up, but talked into his hands, towards the floor. "Adolescents. A whole damned race of adolescents," And in his mind he saw the glories of Earth; the cities stood there in his thoughts with all their towering buildings and their rushing beetle-cars and their overhead railways. The spaceports were there, too, with the rockets soaring upwards and shimmering like silver pencils as they came into land. And Newscreen was there, glowing its messages, its pictures, telling the world of all the great and wonderful things that men were doing.

Men. Nothing but a handful of adolescents on an isolated planet somewhere in space. Little boys with guns. Little boys who must be dealt with severely at times to prevent them from destroying things and getting up to mischief.

No. No. He couldn't believe it. There must be some mistake, something wrong with the Time Brain, perhaps—or perhaps the travelling through time had unhinged Waring's mind. Perhaps, even, the whole thing had been a dream on the part of the crew of the *Sunderling* and Waring had contacted that dream because it had the greater reality for the dreamers. Perhaps any of those things. Any and all of them were preferable to *this!*

Swiftly he turned to the President and to the others, questioning, pleading.

No. It was true, all true.

"But how can you be so sure that it is true?"

The President spoke. "We have previous experience of this, don't forget. At about the time your Caligula was ruling on Earth our scientists had devised a method of reaching the stars. We sent four ships off, one after the other. None came back. During the following eight centuries many more ships were sent. Once more none came back.

"Then our scientists started experimenting with fourth dimensional physics. Our approach was different to yours. We started off with a belief in the psychic plane. Our fourth dimensional research developed through the years. Very soon after the time your world was beleaguered by Adolf

Hitler we came into contact with the Planners on the fourth dimensional plane. We learned the secrets of the stars and learned also that probably within a few hundred years we would be considered fit enough for interstellar travel. Because of our contact with you none of this has ever been entered in any Martian histories that you have been able to obtain. Had we told your race of the Planners when our rockets first landed on Earth no one would have believed us. Similarly had we told you that your first interstellar flight would end in failure you would not have listened. Now one of your race has seen what happened. There can be no further doubting now."

Wade looked at each of the Martians in turn. His eyes were straining to see in their faces something of the terror that he felt. "You have all known of the Planners? And it has not mattered to you? Don't you feel *anything?*"

Yyrmac smiled. "Perhaps we see it differently now to the way our ancestors must have seen it when first the Planners were discovered. Now we merely feel proud, knowing that we are nearer than ever to being judged mature. *We* shall not see interstellar flight, but our descendants will."

"But the feeling that you are no more than puppets! Doesn't that affect you in any way?" Wade's fingers shook. His voice came hoarsely through the laboratory. The thunder had gone out of it, all the power gone. It was a hollow shell of a voice holding itself up by sheer will power.

The President pointed a blue hand up at the crystal roof.

They all looked up.

"They are not demons, up there, you know," he said. "Whatever they are or are not, one thing we know. They are just. And that is the important thing. Your man Waring has told you of the screen pictures of the future that were shown to the crew of the *Sunderling*. Some of our scientists, too, have seen those pictures—or pictures similar to them showing the effects of Martians gaining the stars and the planets of the stars before reaching maturity. Those things are not pleasant to look upon. True they are only possibilities, we know that. Nevertheless they are there in the patterns of the future. No, Wade. Those creatures are not demons."

Wade stood up, his eyes on Waring. "All true," he murmured to himself. "All true."

Waring nodded, straightening himself on the couch, rubbing his eyes as though by so doing he could erase forever the memory of what he had seen.

"Why did you not tell us something—why didn't you warn us that your own ships had failed to come back from outer space?" queried Wade.

The President shrugged slim, blue shoulders. "It would not have done any good. You would still have gone on. There were plenty of people on your own planet who thought that the *Sunderling* was doomed before she started off. They held that Henessey's mathematics were based on wrong premises. They were wrong in that, but they were right in their prophecies about the fate of the ship."

"No, it would have been useless to warn you. We have watched your race and its progress with interest, Wade. We are older than you are as a race. Much older. It is only natural that we should take an interest in your doings. Purposely we have kept ourselves to ourselves and not interfered, for each race must work out its own form of salvation. That is the reason that we did not warn you when we heard that you were going to try for the stars. It is also the reason that we never told you about the Planners. You would not have listened, anyway."

In spite of himself, Wade smiled. It was so true. So very true. Humanity was always right—according to humanity!

No one would have listened to the Martians' warnings. No one on Earth ever *did* listen to warnings.

"There is another point, also," the President went on. "We have, as I say, watched your progress. We are not Planners and have not got the minds or the abilities of the Planners, but we can judge another race by what we see of it. Or perhaps I should say that we can *understand* another race by what we see of it. We have watched your race very closely. As you have been told, the Planners imagine that within a few centuries you will destroy yourselves. Well, that may be. We cannot argue with the Planners, I suppose. Nevertheless, I feel they are wrong. We have watched humanity, as I have said. We have seen its many errors, its many failures. And we have seen its successes. The fact that you bridged interplanetary space when you did proves that technically you are capable of great things. We think the time is not far off when your mental development will be almost as great as ours. Again I say—we are not the Planners. They *know*. We can only judge.

"But you must have read our history. If you have taken the trouble to work out comparative scales of development, you will see that it took us far longer to reach the stage where interplanetary flight was possible than it did your race. True we helped you in your quest for powerful fuels, but eventually you would have found one for yourselves. The Planners say that you are an adolescent race. Well, perhaps they are right. Perhaps you are adolescent. But you are really adolescent prodigies, technically at any rate. And soon, I think, soon you will grow into adults. Much sooner than we ever did."

Wade smiled without meaning to. It was good to hear the Martian President speaking thus. Very good. "I hope you're right," he said. Then his face clouded. He saw Waring looking at him and he remembered his description of the Planners, Robots, Metal men existing in the fourth dimension. Yet how could that be? The fourth dimension was apparently in the psychic plane. How could robots exist *there?*

He looked across at the President. "Tell me," he said, "what is your explanation of the Planners?"

"Explanation?"

"Yes, what do you think they are? How can robots exist in the fourth dimension?"

The President shook his head. "I have no idea. That is a problem that has baffled Martian scientists and thinkers since they first became aware that there was a fourth dimension. Certain of our specialists think that the mass of a body, when reduced in size in the three known dimensions, expands into the fourth. Thus a race that had the knowledge to contract the molecules and atoms of its body into the sub-atomic would expand in the fourth dimension. That is one view. There are as many others as I have fingers on my hands. And so far as I see there is no way to find out. When our people come into contact with the Planners on the fourth dimension there is naturally no talk of such things. For a start the Planners would not tell us, and also—I doubt if they could."

"What do you mean by that?"

"Exactly what I say. These creatures are robots set up to watch over the universe. Would a robot be likely to know what manner of creature designed it?"

"No, I suppose not."

"Of course not. They have volunteered no information, except that they *are* mechanical. That is obvious enough by just looking at them."

On the couch Waring grinned, his mouth splitting open inanely. "*Very* obvious," he said. "Once you had seen that face—oh, God!"

"No doubt at all?" There was a faint hope in Wade's voice.

"No doubt at all."

"I see." The hope was gone.

In another part of the building the generators hummed, mournfully, dully, their sound coming like a funeral dirge, rising and falling.

"So now you have your story for Newscreen," said the President.

Wade laughed. "You think we could run a thing like that?"

"That's what I want to know." said the President.

Wade looked at him in silence for a minute. Then he said, "You suggest we *do* run it?"

"Yes, I suggest you do."

"But for Heaven's sake—imagine what would happen! We should have panics all over Earth."

"Would you? I rather doubt it. Think back to your twentieth century. What happened about the Flying Saucers? It took your people a long time to believe that such things existed. It took them a long time to believe that the Martians were sending them and another long time to believe that the Martians had landed on Earth and made contact with humanity. By the time they accepted these facts everyone on Earth knew that there were Martians and that they were not enemies, but merely another race, albeit different but still just another race. If you run this story on Newscreen you will probably have the same results."

Wade ran his hand round the inside of his collar. His fingers stuck to the sweat on his neck. "What's your interest in all this? Of course, I appreciate your paternal interest as the older planet, but unless I'm mistaken there's, another side to it as well?"

The President nodded. "There is," he said.

The Martians rustled themselves interestedly. "Well, what is it?"

"We are anxious to find out whether we are right in our judgment of your race. Not just from a scientific curiosity or intellectual interest, either. We have kept ourselves to ourselves as you know. That has been done for a very special reason. We think it is best that races in different stages of evolution should not try to influence each other too much. However, we feel that the attitude humanity adopts to this problem—providing that Newscreen runs the story—will tell us more about whether or not your race is adolescent. We do not really feel it is. The Planners think so, obviously. Yet we feel otherwise. It is very presumptuous of us to think so, no doubt, but we do. As I said before—we think you are adolescent prodigies."

"What good will it do you?" Wade asked.

"Perhaps none for a hundred years or so. But if you outstrip us in your progress after that time..."

Wade laughed. "It's flattering to hear you speak in that way. After being told we were little boys with guns it s very flattering."

The President nodded. "I see your point," he said. Never think that the Martians are such complete humanitarians as to ignore anything that might be of benefit to themselves. We are much the same as your own race in many respects, you know."

Wade's eyes travelled once more up to the crystal roof and the stars beyond, as they had done when first he entered the laboratory. There they were—the stars, twinkling their twinkling smiles millions of miles away. Untouchable for another few centuries.

"How can I run the story?" he asked. "Newscreen relays pictures—or texts when pictures aren't available. No one would believe this story if only texts were shown on our screens."

"That is easily arranged." The President looked oddly pleased with himself. "We can help you there. Our mental-films can be operated by telepathic means. Someone can live the story of the *Sunderling* once more through the Time Brain, and their experiences can be transferred onto mentalfilm. You can then use the mentalfilm for your Newscreens."

Thought of the Planners came again into Wade's mind. He saw imaginary pictures of the robots that Waring had described. "What of the Planners?" he asked. "If they are able to see everything, then they will know that we have travelled back in time and have seen the fate of our ship. If they can see all these things, then they will surely prevent us showing Newscreen pictures of that voyage."

The President shook his head. "I rather think not. I think instead that they will watch with much interest. If the results of showing the films are as I foresee, then they will be pleased. If the films produce panics then the Planners' idea that you are all adolescents will be strengthened. I do not think that they will interfere. But that is something that you will have to risk."

Wade grunted. "I'll risk it," he said.

"Then you intend to run the story?"

"Yes."

The President smiled, slowly at first; then his face split in a wide grin, rare indeed for a Martian. "I am more pleased than I can tell you," he said.

Wade hardly heard him. He was looking once again up at the stars. "A race of robots," he whispered. "Who built them, and when, and why?"

"Perhaps when we are adult races we shall know," said the President. There was laughter in his voice.

How can they treat it so lightly wondered Wade? But then they have known about the Planners for so long. Perhaps familiarity does breed contempt. He found that he had spoken the last sentence out loud.

"I wouldn't say that," said the President. "Rather does it breed *familiarity*. We feel we know the Planners now. They are no longer vague shadows ruling our lives. We have come to accept them simply as beings that exist. Nothing more. They do not interfere with us because we have recognized that they are there not to hinder us nor yet to help us, merely to watch us."

"And who made the Planners?" whispered Wade, hardly hearing the President's voice. "How adult does a race have to be before *that* is explained?"

Nobody answered.

Wade and Waring and Van Carlsberg left Mars that same night. They were taken back to Earth in a Martian plane and they landed in the bright daylight some time after.

On Earth it was bright and sunny as the rocket came down to land. It was bright with the morning brilliance coming from a brilliant, friendly sun.

The three men filled their lungs with the good air as they stepped onto the landing field.

Spacemen were walking here and there. Civilians, too.

"What a story we have to tell them," said Wade. "What a story!"

But there was no life in his voice as he spoke. No life at all.

CHAPTER TWELVE
All This Could Happen

AFTER watching the ship cut its way up into the sky, Yyrmac turned to the President. "I wonder what the result will be, sir?" he said.

The President shook his head, his eyes still following the red trail of the rocket. "I don't know," he said, slowly. "I have no doubt that Wade will run the story. Whether the Earthmen believe it or not is another matter. I should imagine, also, that Wade will run into trouble with his Government should they find out the nature of the story he intends to run."

"But providing that he *does* run the story, sir. What then? What do you think will happen? Do you think the Earthmen will believe what they see?"

"That I couldn't say. I rather think they will be divided, some believing, others not. There may be panics, there may not, but whatever happens we shall have tested whether the Earthmen really are as adolescent as the Planners imagine. I do not think they are."

The Martians walked away from the spaceport buildings towards their waiting cars. The night was thinning towards dawn, pale grey light filtering over the distant mountains, the stars fading away in the skies.

At the door of his car the President paused to have a few further words with Yyrmac. "If the Earthmen accept the existence of the Planners and so prove that they are not such babes after all, then we shall be able to cooperate with them freely. They are a young and vigorous race and we are old.

There may well come a time when we shall be pleased to be friendly with Earth. And that time may not be too far away."

All about him the buildings and the roads, glittering now in the dawn light, gave off their perfume of age. The towers and the minarets glowed as they had glowed ten thousand years without change. And it was almost as though the ghosts of earlier towers and minarets were there, too. "All old," said the President, a little sadly.

Then the Martians got into their sleek, golden cars and went off down the white roads, the cars a flight of golden bees traversing an ancient hive.

It was dark.

In Newscreen Building lights glowed in the Night Wing and in Wade's office. The big man sat at his desk, alone.

He had read the thin golden sheets that the Martian President had given him. Read them over and over. Now he must plan the story that would be seen on every Newscreen in the country. He still wondered whether he was doing the right thing. There might be panics. There might be revolts and violence. Men might take this as a sort of "End-of-the-World" crisis. And if there was violence he would be responsible.

The golden sheets rustled in his hands.

Adolescents, he thought. Nothing but a race of adolescents, and that is the story I must tell the world. Some people will believe right enough. There would be those only too eager to prove the existence of beings who governed man's destiny. And there would be those others, always ready to scoff and smile so smugly. They would view the whole thing as a joke. They would watch the Newscreens and the papers and the cinemas and they would never believe any of it. It would take ten years or so for them slowly, gradually, to accept the Planners. It had been the same with the Flying

Saucers and space flight. Some people were so set in their beliefs that no amount even of positive proof would change them.

He had made an arrangement with the Martian President to return to Mars within the week and live the story of the *Sunderling* through the Time Brain, even as Waring had done. But this time the tale would be recorded on Martian mentalfilm. Until then no word of the *Sunderling*'s fate was to be told to anyone. And he had a week to prepare the announcement and introductory text for the story.

He looked out at the stars. Would he ever be able to look at them again in the same way as before, he wondered? And when the story was told, when Newscreen had shown everyone the secrets of outer space—would others be able to see the stars in the same old way? What of the lovers, wandering in starlight? Would they look up at the familiar constellations in fear? He imagined the neurotics and the nervous people and the lonely ones, too. Brooding at night in secluded rooms, gazing up out of their windows, and thinking, thinking...

This was getting him nowhere.

He walked away from the window quickly. There was a story to be written. The greatest story that the world had ever known and possibly the greatest that it ever *would* know.

At his desk he snapped the dictaphone switch, cleared his throat, and started to speak. The drone of his voice sounded in the stillroom.

After fifteen minutes he stopped and played the recording back. He laughed. How futile it sounded. How absurd, too. He tried again, talking this time for half an hour.

Four more attempts he made and by the time he had finished his voice was croaking. He was tired and he sat limply there, listening to his own words filling the huge office. He felt the tiredness seeping through him like an eel sliding in dark waters, coursing through his limbs and his mind. It was more than a physical tiredness; it ate into him, slowing his thoughts.

The recording ended and from a slot in the scriber machine the printed copy of what he had said dropped onto the waiting plate and slid across the desk towards him.

There it was. The story. Or the first draft, anyway.

He put the recording and the script into the drawer of his desk, locking the drawer afterwards.

Then he went out of the office, down in the elevator and out into the starlit night.

Van Carlsberg and Waring sat in the bar together, with their drinks in front of them and their faces long and melancholy. They had been drinking for some time. There was no one else in the bar and it was near to closing time.

Van Carlsberg looked at his glass, turning it in his hands, watching the spirit slop from one side to the other.

"I can't help thinking about it, you know," he said. "I just can't help it. There doesn't seem anything else left in the world to think about. Nothing except those robots up there *looking* at us. All the time *looking*."

"Yes."

"I suppose I shall always feel it, when I'm in space, too. And I've been through a lot of different parts of space and know the feel of it. But it won't be the same any more. Not now it won't. And I keep thinking about Nolan. I knew him pretty well, you know."

"Uh-huh."

"Pretty well, yes. I keep thinking about what you told Wade—about who would have gone on the *Sunderling* if Nolan hadn't. It might have been me. I might have gone through all that."

Van Carlsberg shuddered and his drink spilled over onto the polished top of the table. Van Carlsberg looked down and saw his face staring blackly up from the pool of spirit. "I'm getting tight," he said. "And I'm going to get tighter."

Waring laughed. "It won't do any good. You won't drown *these* memories. They'll stay with you the same as they'll stay with me."

The door banged. Two men came in. One of them was tall and lean and brown. He looked across.

"Why—Van Carlsberg or I'm a Martian!"

"Hullo, Slade."

"Well, well, quite a surprise. Let me introduce Martin Amery—Captain Van Carlsberg."

Waring was introduced and the two newcomers sat down. More drinks were ordered.

"Heard you were away on some official business. That right?"

Van Carlsberg shook his head. "Holiday. Who told you about 'official business'?"

"Oh, I don't know. Just in from Venus. Heard it somewhere there, I suppose. Man—that planet's *rich*. Mr. Amery here is working on a new form of rocket fuel. I've been taking him over to Venus to investigate the mineral resources there. Mr. Amery thinks that within a very short time we shall have a fuel capable of driving a ship at perhaps *eight or nine times* the present maximum speed!"

"Really?" said Van Carlsberg.

"That's right, isn't it, Mr. Amery?"

"Certainly is."

"Well," said Van Carlsberg. He was thinking of the Planner's words, and he knew that Waring was thinking of them, too. *You have progressed in one direction only. You are like the freak who grows to about nine or ten feet and then finds that his legs can hardly support the weight of his body. Your technical achievements show intensive progress along that single, and narrow, line. But the truth is that you are not yet grown up. You are still in your adolescence. And nobody trusts an adolescent with an atom bomb.*

"Goodnight, gentlemen," said Van Carlsberg, standing up and walking from the table.

The door banged after him.

"Well, what do you think was the matter with him?" asked the two men together.

"I couldn't imagine," said Waring.

Van Carlsberg came out of the bar and looked about him. The bar was on a main street and beetles hummed back and forth, quietly making their way here and there in the city, taking their occupants about their *business!* Van Cads berg laughed. Their business! It had a funny sound, now. The business of children playing at being grown-ups.

He stood for a moment waiting, thinking of what he should do next. Should he go into one of the spaceport bars, where he could drink until morning? Or should he go back to his hotel and try to sleep?

Try to sleep! That was a laugh. How could anyone sleep when he knew about the Planners? And soon everyone would know about them.

A passing beetlecar stopped and a uniformed head poked out of the window. "Can I give you a lift somewhere, Captain?"

A Transport Spaceman. They always know the best bars. "I need a drink," said Van Carlsberg.

"That makes two of us. Jump in."

Waring left the bar soon after Van Carlsberg to make his way homeward. His beetlecar lay in a garage some hundred yards down the street and he walked along towards it, not hurrying, not dawdling. Just walking.

All the terror and the fear of what he had seen had left him now and he felt only a great helplessness, and, when he thought of it he realized that that was probably the best thing he *could* feel. There was no way of fighting against the Planners. They were there and that was that; there was no altering something that had existed millions of years before Earth was born and would exist millions of years after it had become a dead and freezing world.

He tried to think of them as the Martians had described them; not as monsters but as just rulers—or not really even rulers. Gods, perhaps; strange, paternal creatures who watched but did not interfere except in exceptional circumstances.

Briefly he wondered whether the story would be allowed to be run at all. Supposing the Planners decided that it would be harmful for Earth to know—would they remove Wade and Van Carlsberg and himself? Would they alter the patterns so that three men had never existed, never lived at all?

But the Martians knew. The Planners would not remove all the Martians. They had not done so when the Martians explored the fourth dimension, so there was no reason for them to do so now. If they had wanted to prevent the Martians from telling the Earthmen about them they would have done so before now. No. The Planners would let the story be run. The more he thought about it, the more certain he became that he was right.

And that meant that the Planners must have a *certain* faith in the Earthmen for all their talk of adolescence. Or did it merely mean that they were not concerned with preventing the Earthmen from destroying themselves providing that the destruction did not extend outside the Solar System.

There was no end to the questions. No end."

He reached the garage and got his beetlecar from the lock-up.

Driving back along the white road home he started to think of what Jo would say when the story came out on the Newscreens. He would not tell her until then, of course. She never asked him about any of his assignments until he was ready to tell her.

The thought of Jo and the babes made him drive faster. The beetlecar chewed at the white snake of the road, humming to itself as it did so.

He turned down familiar roads, swerving this way and that. Soon the bungalow came into sight.

He gave a long whistle. Lights appeared in the front room and the curtains drew back. In a moment Jo was running down the drive towards him.

The Planners were considering the case of the third planet of the sun known as Sol.

In blackness divorced from all time and space they communicated with each other.

"The patterns give many probabilities and an infinity of possibilities. There is no way of telling. The chances are about balanced."

"But at their stage of development it would be wrong for them to know about us."

"It would be even more wrong if we were to interfere."

"We are not here to govern these creatures," said a third. "We are here to watch."

"I still think we should prevent their knowing. It could be done quite simply. There are only three men and their relatives who would have to be removed from Earth. Others could be set in their place. No one would know. As for the Martians—we simply remove the *wish* to tell the Earthmen about us, that is all. We also naturally remove all knowledge of what has happened regarding the *Sunderling* and the Time Brain."

"Do we also remove knowledge of the *Sunderling* itself from the Martians and the Earthmen? Can you not see how *much* would be altered?"

There was a silence among the Planners.

"Then they will be allowed to tell the story and know about us?"

"Surely that is the only way. The probabilities are that they will accept us and, like the Martians, will eventually attempt to reach mental adulthood, consciously strive for it. I mean."

"That is only one probability. The others?"

The Planners searched the future, seeing there the inter-changing patterns, the weaving of the multiple threads of the future.

The probabilities showed panic, death, revolution, chaos.

"You think that we should risk that?"

"We have risked things before."

"Yes—look at Marthon, seventh planet of the sun Keramin. A dead world because we took a risk, gambled on a race reaching adulthood in just such Circumstances as these."

"But look at Nomool. The races there are among the most advanced throughout the universe. We took a chance *there*, too."

"So be it then."

In the blackness beyond all things the Planners turned their minds away from Earth. A new system of planets was to be formed. They must plan the life that was to walk it a billion billion years hence. In another part of the universe a race had discovered a means of bridging interplanetary space by telepathic means. Their minds were basically evil and the corruption was spreading, spreading through the twenty-eight planets of that vast system. There was work to be done there, too.

On Earth life ticked itself away, and a race of adolescents ate their meals, dreamed their dreams, walked their walks, flew their flights, thought their thoughts.

And the hands of life's great clock moved onwards, inexorably, towards one or other of the infinity of possibilities or the fewer probabilities, one of which would be Earth's future.

THE END